I0584078

Metaphorosis

September 2021

Beautifully made speculative fiction

Also from Metaphorosis

Metaphorosis

September 2021

edited by
B. Morris Allen

ISSN: 2573-136X (online)
ISBN: 978-1-64076-207-7 (e-book)
ISBN: 978-1-64076-208-4 (paperback)

Metaphorosis
a magazine of speculative fiction
from
Metaphorosis Publishing

Neskowin

September 2021

Tumbler...7
    by B. Morris Allen

Till All the Hundred Summers Pass.........35
    by J.A. Legg

A Seedling in the Dark............................97
    by Eleanor R. Wood

The Nocturnals V...................................135
    by Mariah Montoya

Tumbler

B. Morris Allen

A spider hung across from me, the barbed spikes of its legs dug deep into the walls of its prison. It was caged in a network of tunnels and tubules that wrapped around and through each other in an immense tangle. Trapped. Just like me.

I freed a leg and waved at it. They never waved back. Something drove me to keep trying, some visceral urge to communicate, to share more than just "Good fungus this way" or "Break in the tunnel ahead". I did a little dance, to show I wasn't just stretching. I lifted each leg in turn, sending a ripple of motion around my perimeter. It was a pointless risk, and yet it felt good, and I sent the ripple around again and again. *This is forever,* the ripple said. *Though it starts and stops, though it is incomplete, this is a cycle capable of endless repetition.*

The other fixed its eyestalks on me, but made no move. Perhaps metaphysics is too much to ask from a simple dance.

In the Out, white scudded across the blue. Soon, we would roll. I could feel it in the flexing of the tubes, in the shifts across the tangle. In its tubule, the other spider bobbed back and forth with the flex. Or I did. We came closer, tantalizingly close, the transparent walls of our tubules almost touching, our bodies almost belly to belly across the distance. Then the flex pulled us apart again, and we were rolling. As we parted, I saw the other raise one leg, then another, in a clumsy imitation of my dance. And then it lost its hold with the roll, and it wrapped its legs around it in a tough, chitinous ball that rattled away down the tubes toward the ever-shifting bottom.

I watched it go, until distance and tunnel walls obscured it from view. It had answered, or tried to. I was sure of it. Why else let go so close to a roll? *Because the fungus was exhausted*, common sense answered. *Because it was frightened of your strangeness*, said my own fear.

Because it understood, hope responded. *Because it too wants more than this endless maze. Wants purpose, wants togetherness.*

What togetherness consisted of, I wasn't sure. Someone I could talk with about the hazy, half-formed dreams that came to me while I digested, the drive that had led me to learn to dance, to turn jerky, unnatural motion into a smooth, gliding celebration of freedom.

I wanted to fold my legs in, to pull my head in and curl into a ball and let gravity take me where it would through the tunnels, to proclaim my happiness by letting nature have its way with me. I could feel my tip segments flexing with the desire to let go. But if I did, how would the other ever find me?

Instead, I clung like a mite to a spore body, too young to know the world, too soft to survive it. I clung, and I waited.

Our roll was a short one. The tangle fetched up against a boulder in the Out, and though wind pushed us to and fro, we were fixed in place once more, until the wind should shift.

My loop of the tangle had fetched up near the top, the curves of the tube slanting down to both sides. Above me, the blue was achingly clear, only accentuated by wisps of white floating away to the unknown. They moved slowly, like a spiderling just learning to crab its way across the walls and past the dense mycelium of the spore body. Were the white things tangles, I wondered? Distant relatives of our own, but unbound from the soil of the surface, and with spiders of their own living amongst the white?

I would never know. No one would. We were trapped here, all of us, in the endless labyrinth of clear walls and soft surfaces.

Eating always makes me feel better. I released my barbs and scuttled across to the mat of fungus that had brought me here in the first place. To my under-eyes, it was even juicier than it had first appeared, and I gathered it eagerly with my mandibles, ripping out hunks and passing them to my mouth for ingestion. Other spiders avoided these outer paths, but the warm light that made them feel strange invigorated me. It had made me larger than most, my outer shell tougher, more rigid. There were paths in the interior where I could no longer pass, like a spiderling barred forever from the spore bodies that had borne it, its hard body no longer welcome in the cushioning moss of the spore beds.

It didn't matter to me. Out here, the fungus was richer, the light brighter. And there was the Out — the fascinating reach of plains and gullies, of boulders and trees, those strange creatures with their straight trunks, and wild, tangle-like tops that swayed in the wind, but never rolled away.

'Watch for the Out!' was the cry that came down the passageways at times. 'Break ahead! Cling tight!' And we let those tunnels fill with fungus until they healed or closed entirely. Because to approach the Out was to be lost forever, to never feel the roll of wind again, to be left behind, exposed and alone.

You can be alone in the tangle, said my contrary mind. *You are alone*, said my heart.

I wasn't, though. Before a day had passed, that other spider was back. It was the same, I was sure. It had been a Seven, its strong, thick limbs a sharp contrast to my own more fragile nine. And the scarlet swirls across the upper carapace that had reminded me of a tree shedding its tangle were the same.

It settled itself on the wall of the tunnel opposite, clinging to the far side, so that its upper-eyes could stare across at me. I scuttled up to a similar position and waved.

It watched me. I imagined the climb it must have had, from wherever the roll had flung it. It would be tired. And uncertain whether what it had seen was a message, or just a spider in the throes of mold-sickness.

I did my circle dance again, once, twice, three times. Then I reversed course, and ran the circle the other way. Three times. No mold-sickness here.

I could see Red Tree cast an eye to the blue above. It was still, with thick sheets of white layered on each other like a fungus mat not touched for weeks. With a slow, tentative motion, Red Tree raised one leg, planted it deliberately. Lifted another leg, planted it. Then another. With each leg, it moved quicker, more surely, until at last its dance was a slow, stately, seductive ripple. Once, twice, thrice around.

I did a little dance of my own, a formless, bouncing swirl of jubilation. At last! After countless weeks of blank stares, I had a partner in my mania at last. I raised two legs to it in a salute. After a moment, it raised its own. The two of us, reaching out to each other across the gap, across the tubes. Pointless, unless we met.

And yet, how could we? The tangle was a maze of tubes that wove in and out, that crossed and knotted, and occasionally connected. But where? I had never given much thought to it, had never tried to map the tangle beyond In and Out, core and edge, up and down, and those latter changed with ever roll, every shift.

Here, we could see each other, could dance for each other and ourselves. It was more than I had ever really hoped for. And already it was not enough. Already, I longed to touch the other, to feel the hard gloss of Red Tree's shell beneath my barbs, to talk, to ask my questions that had no answers.

I looked through my tubule, across the gap. I could see where Red Tree's tube curved up to the left, to where it entered a dense knot of threads that promised narrow passages and tight spaces. Too tight for me, and perhaps even for Red Tree, with its smaller, stiffer Seven body.

To the right, Red Tree's tube spun down into a coil that wrapped around several others before diving briefly toward the core and then lifting back out — toward me! And my own right hand tunnel sank down in a similar direction.

I lifted one leg, then, two, then a daring three, and pointed them, waved them all to the right. *Go right*, I urged with all the power in me. *Meet me — there.*

Red Tree raised a leg. Not one of those on the right, however. Instead, it waved it up and down, in a languid motion, like a spiderling testing its balance. Then it scuttled forward, up the near side of its tube, until its underside faced me, and its under-eyes emerged to to give what was no doubt a blurry picture at such distance.

We marked walls from time to time, of course, scratches at the intersections, a few symbols that meant 'Break' or 'Fungus' or 'Danger! Water!'. But those were superficial, and lasted only a day or two before the walls healed. I'd never seen such deliberate damage, damage that would take weeks to regrow, or even months. A careless jab might even let water in, and with it the strand-sickness that could turn a spider's legs to useless, ductile sprigs of bristle.

Regardless of the danger, Red Tree raised another leg, plunged it in and ripped out another chunk of wall, over and over until a rough circle of divots surrounded it. I'd never seen anything like it.

When it was done at last, Red Tree gave a two-legged salute, then backed down to the floor of its tunnel, where it could see me with its upper-eyes.

It seemed to be waiting for something. Was this a dance of its own, I wondered? Its own celebration of life, of risk?

It seemed impatient. It raised its nearest leg, waved it in my direction, then raised it and slowly, pointedly, lowered it to the floor, barbs extended. I watched as it repeated the motion.

It had repeated my dance. It seemed only polite that I should do the same. I scuttled up to the tunnel wall closest to Red Tree. From my under-eyes, I could see no more than a vague shape, a blob of red and black across the way. I could see the wall of the tunnel much more clearly. It was bare here of fungus, which tended to grow on the inner, more protected

surfaces. The wall was thick, its tough
outer rind barely visible through a softer,
more flexible inner surface the depth of
my shortest legs. Mine was a tube in
middle age, still growing, still well
nourished from the core, with feeder hairs
that picked up moisture when it was at
the bottom, and blocked some of the
harsher light when it was at the top like
now.

It was a healthy tube, in other words,
unlikely to crack open no matter what I
did to it. I was safe from the Out, would
be taking no chances. I raised a leg
tentatively, and saw Red Tree bounce in
satisfaction. I thrust the spike of my leg
hard into the wall. It sank in smoothly to
the first joint, and my barbs came out
instinctively, anchoring me against
unexpected turbulence. I withdrew the
barbs and pulled the leg out.

I saw immediately that it wasn't having
the desired effect, that the spike simply
withdrew as smoothly as it had gone in,
just as it was designed to do; as it had
always done before. Across the way, Red
Tree hunkered down in disappointment,
as I read it.

I stopped, and pushed the leg back in. I
had never reused a spike hole this way. It

felt strange, the gel of the wall giving way before my spike, almost welcoming it. I extended my barbs again, and pulled. I pulled tentatively at first, uncertain. But the barbs held as they were meant to, and the material of the wall refused to give way. I pulled harder, and harder, until I began to feel a pain in my joint. It grew and grew, until it felt as if the leg would part, the way they sometimes do in really terrible storm rolls. It had only happened to me a few times, but it hurt — a lot — and took weeks to regrow.

Across from me, I could see Red Tree with my under-eyes, a blurry figure doing something with a near leg. I ignored it and went back to my pulling.

The strain was worse, and I felt as if I'd done something to the joint. It hurt worse now, and the barbs were moving less, if possible.

The barbs! Red Tree had partially retracted its barbs, I remembered. Of course it had. I laughed and bobbed as I realized. My joint hurt, but I gleefully raised another leg and plunged it into the wall. With a smooth motion, I retracted the barbs almost all the way and jerked it loose. It felt unnatural, this half-in, half-out position, but the barbs cooperated, and the leg ripped loose from the wall along with a satisfying crumble of wall material.

It made an unsightly, distinctive mark, and suddenly I understood. The mark was the point of it all. Red Tree had marked its tube so that it would know where our meeting point was, and now I had done the same with mine. The tubes would shift a little, with time, but now we knew where our initial meeting place had been. At least in this one place, we were close enough to see each other, to communicate in the limited way we had. I gave Red Tree a two-legged salute, then went back to my marking, working all around my perimeter, in a violent version of my circle dance, until I was surrounded by my own ring of divots. They would take weeks to heal. Where once that would have filled me with an unnamed dread, now I felt only warm satisfaction. No longer the telltale sign of a risk of the Out, this ring was my mark. Mine and Red Tree's.

I crabbed back down to the floor of the tunnel, where I could deploy my upper-eyes. Red Tree saluted with two precise legs, then pointed off to the right, to where our tubes might meet. I did the same, and with slow, excited purpose, we set off.

We lost sight of each other soon enough. My tunnel was unfrequented, and hazed with fungus across most of its breadth. Not thick, but enough to obscure my vision. When I paused to eat a space clear, I found the fungus tough and chewy, the result of infrequent harvesting that ate away the juicy upper layers and left the thick lower ones alone. When I'd cleared a fair portion, I crept away and looked through with my upper-eyes. I could see what I thought was Red Tree's tube, angling away now toward the core, while mine traveled perpendicular, along the middle surface.

It wasn't long before I reached an intersection, a place where tubules had grown close enough that their walls had merged, and the interior barriers atrophied to nothing. One of the ways led down toward the core, and I turned to follow it with joy.

I had gone only a few bodylengths when I turned back. Red Tree had taught me to mark my way, and I returned to the intersection. The new tube was younger, thinner, but more pliable. I settled for a shallower trio of marks, pointing back the way I'd come, like the spike of a thick leg pulling out of the wall.

Toward the wall, I told myself. *You come from the wall, go back toward the wall.* It should be enough. If I could remember to look. I crawled away down the new tunnel, mind tight with discipline, heart warm with adopted cleverness.

I wandered for a week before I came back to the surface. We had rolled this way and that, and I'd spent a whole day, once, clinging tight to a tunnel while a storm flung the tangle around, battering us against rocks and trees until tubules broke on every hand, and deadly water found its way into the tunnels. Spiders crawled frantically one way and another to avoid rivulets, rills, and even puddles until the walls could absorb it all. When the rain stopped at last, a gale rolled us on, and spider after spider fell through the gaps into the Out. I was tired and bruised by the time I found my way back to my ring of divots.

I had mapped extensively since I left, from the surface toward the core, from the loose, dangerous outer paths to the tight, constricting inner ones. Half my paths had broken open, it seemed, and it had taken me days to find alternate routes. In none of them had I seen any sign of Red Tree.

Yet here it was, waiting by its own ring of divots, in the tunnel across from me. The tubes were nearer each other now, and I could see it more clearly. The swirls of red looked less like a tree now, more random, and I thought Red Tree itself looked larger. Perhaps it had spent its time nearer the surface, while I had been forcing my way into the smaller inner tunnels.

I saluted it, and shrugged. *What now?*

It climbed over next to its mark, and made several more. They looked like a square with a point at the top, pointing toward the divots.

I understood it, this time. I climbed up and made my own triangle of marks, pointing toward my divots, then climbed back down. Our signatures. I had seen plenty of marks in my wandering, but none of Red Tree's. A shrug from across the way said it had not seen mine.

Was this all there was? Had we found each other, spent so much effort, only to have it come to nothing, to nothing more than vague philosophy across the distance? *This dance is forever*, my mind mocked bitterly.

Red Tree was dancing anyway. It was a complex sequence, full of stops and starts and circles and shifts, with sometimes one leg in motion, sometimes two or three or four, and I marveled at Red Tree's bravery. We were at rest, our tubes low on the side of the tangle, but a wind might roll us at any moment, and with only three legs holding, Red Tree would be forced to ball up and let fate have its way.

It took time, but eventually I thought I understood. Red Tree had found a distinctive intersection, where a total of five tubules crossed and merged in a complex pattern. It suggested we should try to meet there, or near there. With so many intersections, our odds of success should improve.

I had seen no such cluster, but the idea of a definite target gave me hope. And it was something I could ask about. I had tried, in my travels, to ask about Red Tree, but the other spiders seemed confused by the notion. 'Some spiders are red and black,' they had said. 'Some are green and black, like you.' We had gotten no further than that.

I bobbed up and down to signal assent, but Red Tree was not finished. I caught on quicker this time. With much awkward stretching and stroking of eyestalks, it indicated that it had only *seen* the intersection, but not yet reached it. Nonetheless, it seemed a good target.

Somewhere *that* way, it indicated, with a leg jabbed toward the interior and the upper left. Direction could be tricky in the tangle, I'd found. The tubules wrapped and twisted so much that no direction remained constant for long, but for coreward and surfaceward, and In and Out.

We spent the day resting and eating, and occasionally dancing. We communicated nothing but joy and partnership, and longing, but it was enough. I crept as close to the wall as I could, and watched Red Tree hungrily, forming the scarlet spirals on its shell into trees and clouds and fungus and desire. It watched me the same way, both of us reaching out for something more, something that would bring us beyond the pointless maze and give us meaning. When I changed my circle dance, so that instead of just lifting legs, my whole body swirled in a circle, it bobbed and saluted in a three-legged gesture of joy.

The next day, we set off again. I went to the left this time, down the path that seemed to lead away. But I had already learned that the tunnels seldom went where they seemed to. And off to the right, I'd seen no sign of the five tube crossing. This way was as good as any other.

I wandered for two weeks before I came cross a hint of it. I was down toward the core, wedged in as close as I could get, where the spiders were more plentiful, and even spiderlings hesitantly crawled the walls. They shied away from me, as small next to my bulk as our tangle was to a tree.

One spider, though, a mottled yellow Five, knew the intersection.

"Yes," it said, after we'd given up on any explanation of why it was important. "This tunnel. That way." It waved a leg. "Old tunnels, fragile." Answer given, it scuttled off in search of fresh fungus.

I followed the tunnel it indicated, waiting at every intersection until a spider passed by who knew the way. I found three way intersections, and a four way intersection, but not five, and I began to despair, thinking that perhaps one guide or another had simply miscounted. But to a spider, four is an unnatural number. It's hard to confuse with five. I still had hope.

Yet it was with surprise that one day I suddenly found myself in the intersection itself. I'd been wandering slowly, stopping to eat at every opportunity, for fungus was scarce here. The tunnel walls were old and brittle, in some places almost dead, with few of the xylem veins the fungus tapped into. The walls had opaqued with age, a sure sign of malnourishment, and in one perilous place, I had even found a leg-sized hole right through the wall to the Out. It had been a dry day, but I'd passed the place by as quickly as I could manage, ignoring the intriguing scents that flooded the tunnel nearby.

The memory of those scents had stayed with me — the tantalizing richness of the air, the fearful feel of moisture, the shuddery sense of Out coming In.

I had stopped at a three-way intersection to rest and mark my way. That done, I wandered into the new tunnel, searching for fungus, when I realized that the new tunnel intersected another, and that that one crossed yet another. Five tunnels! Five tubules intersecting! This was it, or at least its double, and I'd seen no other such intersection in all my wandering.

I had made it. It was a strange mix of excitement and disappointment. While I had searched, I had had a goal, a purpose. Now that I had reached that goal, I had nothing again. Red Tree was not here, and though I searched and searched, there was no sign that it had been here. The fungus was sparse and tough and hardly worth harvesting. The whole region was so rickety that it felt unsafe even to sit here with all nine legs dug into the wall. The walls themselves felt so thin they might be pierced by a careless spike, and they were so opaque that that I could barely see a body length outside them.

But I was here. Red Tree would come. It should be here already, in fact, for it had known of the intersection before. But only from a distance, I reminded myself. It had seen the intersection from outside. Which meant it had been in a newer, more transparent tubule.

I flung myself into the search again, looking now for fresh nearby tubules.

Heedless of risk, I sought out the thin
spots in old walls, where their scarred
opacity was offset by attenuated frailty.
There was barely enough to hold onto
here, but I could see. Toward the end of
the second day, I found it —— a clear, thin
window of tubule from which I could see a
familiar red and black shape, legs waving
welcome.

I returned from another fruitless
exploration to find Red Tree already
waiting. Not only waiting, but marking,
ripping out chunk after chunk of wall with
a fervor that made me worry for its sanity.
We were near the top of the tangle today,
and I could see from the dark clouds
above that a storm was on its way — a
wild thing that could pick up our tangle
and throw it bodily through the air. I
would have to move away to find a safe
spot to shelter, away from these friable
walls and their risk of the Out. I had come
by only for a few more moments close to
Red Tree.

It continued its assault on the tunnel
walls, well past a circle now. With every
pull of barbed leg, a larger chunk of wall

material ripped out, until it was clinging to a veritable pit, its body so deep in the wall that its head was flush with the surface. And still it kept digging.

Red Tree had already demonstrated that it was smarter than I was, or more intuitive. It wasn't until it plunged a spike all the way through the outer wall that I finally understood. It was cutting through. If we could not find our way to each other through the tunnels, it would come to me across the Out.

I could feel my flesh creep away from my shell inside me. To go to the Out, deliberately! Knowing the risk. Knowing it might never come back. And all because I had danced.

The moment seemed to stretch for days, but perhaps it was only moments before I too was attacking my wall. The old material chipped away easily, but in tiny flakes. Across the way, I could see Red Tree's scratched, battered spikes cutting through the wall of its tunnel, ripping away long shreds of glassy fiber.

Around us, the roar of the wind picked up as the storm reached us. Within moments, we were rolling, tumbling this way and that, and bouncing high into the air one moment, crashing down onto the plain the next. Through it all, we continued our assault — Red Tree tearing its hole wider and wider with its barbs, and I throwing myself bodily against the wall until I was covered with a dusting of powder and flakes.

The storm worsened, and I began to fear that the rain would come before we finished, before we made the crossing. I'd seen a spider with the thread-sickness once from stumbling into a storm leak, and it had been pitiful. Unable to grip the walls, unable to roll into a proper ball, it had been battered to pieces by the roll of the tangle. I didn't want that to happen to Red Tree, or to me.

The rain held off, but the wind began to howl, and the pressure through the holes we'd carved made it even harder to hold on. But we did, and at last the holes were big enough for Red Tree's smaller body. I forced my way as far into my hole as I could, stretching four legs across the gap, with four more inside, and one more braced on the outside of the tube. It was surprisingly rough and hard, not like the soft gel of the interior. But it gave a good grip, and that was all I cared about.

Across the way, Red Tree bobbed a few times, then gave a quick salute, and jumped. I think it jumped. I'd never seen a spider jump before, but Red Tree was a wild one; it had already proved that. Perhaps it was only the roll of the tangle, or the jolt of the wind, but I like to think it jumped.

In any case, before I knew it, it was on me, its shell hard next to mine, smooth and glossy as seven legs scrabbled for purchase. I threw my four outer legs around it, tangling awkwardly with its own, and extending my barbs in desperation as I felt it slip, slip away.

I felt Red Tree's own barbs extending, felt one catch in a knee joint, then another, forced my own spike through one of its legs as well, until we were locked together as tightly as a mite swathed in a spore body.

And then the storm ripped us loose. A gust of wind threw the tangle high in the air, and slammed it down hard on a boulder. I felt a leg tear loose at the joint, felt Red Tree fall away.

I didn't stop to think, to fear. I pushed with all my inside legs and felt a part of my shell crack as I forced it through the outer wall. The storm lifted the tangle, and we fell, away from it, into the Out.

We landed hard. I felt two more legs break, and the crack in my shell widened. When I put out an upper-eye, I could see all the way through my shell, into the soft flesh of my interior. It struck me how much I was like the tangle, in a way — supple on the inside, tough on the outside. And now my inside was out, and I was too.

"I liked your dance," said Red Tree, and I whirled my eye stalks toward it. It lay next to me, its beautiful red-black shell still whole, the abstract swirls more beautiful than ever before, even less like a tree than ever, but more like something else, something better, more pure. More Red Tree. All its legs were broken, two of them ripped out completely, and I could see the ichor leaking out of them. Treacherous rills of it wended their way toward the pool that I could see under me with my under-eyes. I watched as they merged into one sickly white puddle.

"You're beautiful," I said.

The rain came down and washed us clean. Already I could feel the thread sickness, and I could see the tendrils creeping out of Red Tree's broken joints. I stretched out three legs, and dragged my way over to it, ignoring the pain in my shell, and the odd, cool feel of the rain pouring into me. I stretched my long limbs over Red Tree's dark shell, ignoring the long hairs that stretched blindly toward the water and the soil below. They dug their way in, and I could feel myself tied down, anchored to the Out, where I would never move again.

"It feels right," Red Tree said, and I didn't have to ask what it meant. It felt right to be here, to be with each other at last, no matter the cost. And it felt right to have the thread-sickness, to feel it tie me closer to the earth. I could feel the water now, feel myself drinking it up through the root tendrils, feel it giving rise to new growth inside me.

Under me, Red Tree's shell began to soften, and I could feel the echo of my own pain inside it — the good pain of change and discovery. Already, a stem was rising from the soft muddle of Red Tree's innards, and I felt one rising in me as well. With a last clumsy thrust of my eye stalk, I pushed my stem to the side, and watched it wind around Red Tree's, in a tangle that might never come free.

See B. Morris Allen's story "Tumbler" online at Metaphorosis.
If you liked it, leave a comment. Authors love that!
Remember to subscribe to our e-mail updates so you'll know when new stories are posted.

About the story

I don't remember the genesis of this story, only that I had the image of people living inside a giant, transparent tumbleweed, able to signal each other, but having to develop a kind of semaphore. It was only later that they turned into spiders, and later yet that I understood what they wanted and how the lifecycles of spider and tumbleweed intertwined.

Till All the Hundred Summers Pass

J.A. Legg

"*Spindle*, this is *Sky Castle*; come in, *Spindle*."

Aurora grabbed a handhold and pulled herself to the front of the command module as the voice came through her headset—the first signal from home the ship had received since travelling back through the wormhole. The first word from Earth in over a year.

Her pulse quickened as she pressed the button on her mic. "This is *Spindle*," she breathed. "Aurora King speaking; how soon until you can bring us home? Over."

She heard the cold slap of palms against rungs in the ladder shaft that led down to the spinning gravity wheel. It was Fairburn, come to relieve her at the end of her seven-hour shift. He thrust himself up the tunnel and grabbed a headset hanging near the entrance. He was a few minutes early, and she thought about clocking out, but Commander Grimm could be pretty rigid about time stamps. She pulled up the map on the monitor in front of her, trying not to look at him. Her muscles tightened.

Fairburn nodded. "Talking to someone?"

"*Sky Castle*," she nodded. "We're in home space. Just short of Neptune's orbit." The *Spindle*'s blue dot blipped toward a green light on the far end of the screen. *Blip. Blip.*

"Almost home," he breathed.

Home. It seemed strange to Aurora, after all she'd been through, to describe Earth that way. Especially since the one thing she had missed—the one thing she really wished she could come back to, the one person that really felt like home—wouldn't be there.

Phil.

The engagement ring he had given her still hung around her neck, and she'd clipped a photo of him to the glass on her ship's berth. They were good reminders—but just reminders. Shadows. Cheap copies of the real Phil. They weren't enough.

Especially because he was *supposed* to be here. On the ship. With her.

"Where's Grimm?" Fairburn asked.

"Dinner break," she answered flatly, careful not to turn her head. "He'll be back soon, I'm sure." She reached down to the communicator clipped to her belt and clicked the pager button. The commander would want to be here when the next word from *Sky Castle* came in.

Fairburn glided through the module's null gravity, then coasted to a stop beside her at the control interface. She fixed her attention forward, away from him.

"*Spindle*, we have a lock on your coordinates and we're sending you our information," came the voice in their headsets. "Can you confirm your trajectory?"

Fairburn scanned the information. "Confirm, *Sky Castle*." He took his hand off the button, then paused before speaking again.

"Will you tell?" he asked.

Tell what you did to him, Fairburn? she thought. *Tell how you took him from me?*

"No," she said at last. Even if she did, it wouldn't change anything. Phil would still be gone.

More silence.

"He's long dead now, you know," Fairburn said.

Aurora glared at him. Her fingers clenched into a fist. "Do you have to?" she rasped.

He turned back to study the interface.

"Look at me," she said, louder.

His finger traced the ship's trajectory across the monitor. He drummed against the edge of the control panel in time with the blue dot flashing on the screen. Her shift ended.

"*Look* at me."

Aurora wrenched his shoulder back so that he faced her, away from the starboard wall. He stared and let the uncomfortable silence hang in the air. She studied him closely, searching for a hint of remorse. Nothing.

Unbelievable.

Somewhere in the back of her mind it registered that Commander Grimm could come back at any moment, but she didn't care. She had had enough. She kicked off from the edge of the control panel and pushed him hard against the far wall, teeth clenched. Fairburn collided with the metal, his face still hard as her blow sent her back toward the module's other side.

"You got what you wanted. I'm here. You're here. And he's not. Isn't that enough?" There was a crack in her voice. *Damn it.*

"*Spindle*?" asked the headset. "Looks like you'll be crossing into our orbit in another twelve hours. We're adjusting course to meet with you then. You'll be home soon."

Fairburn kicked toward the interface. "Confirm, *Sky Castle*," he said. "See you then."

He looked out into the void. The sound of hands on rungs came up again through the tunnel. Grimm was back from dinner.

"I didn't get *every*thing I wanted, Aurora," he told her at last, levelly. "You know that."

Didn't get everything I wanted. She thought back to the offer he'd made her, back on the planet. It still made her stomach turn.

You didn't get me.

"Yeah," she said. "Yeah, well, neither did the rest of us."

The commander emerged into the module. Aurora ignored him and made for the exit. She pushed past Fairburn, past Grimm, swung her body toward the tunnel, then dropped feet-first toward the floor below.

"Not even close."

Aurora had been eleven when she'd first studied NASA's launch of the *Dove* and *Olive* probes through the wormhole nearly a century before. She'd been working on a school project with her dad; he was an amateur astronomer himself, and he knew how to talk about science so that everyone in earshot would love it like he did. Especially Aurora.

She listened in rapt attention as he explained the physics behind the wormhole using one of her mother's crochet needles and a Post-It note. "A wormhole," he said, poking the needle through one side of the paper, "bends space and time so we can travel vast distances and back again quicker than we would ever be able to do without it. Like this." He bent the note around the needle and poked it through the other side. "So fast," he added, "that time actually passes slower on the way through the wormhole than it does on Earth." She'd used the same illustration with her class the following day.

She was thirteen when the probes' data came in to the research base stationed on Triton. *Dove* and *Olive* had sent back a host of new discoveries—chief amongst them a new exoplanet, the fifth in orbit around the star NASA had dubbed Perrault. By the end of five years, the astronomers had reached a consensus: Perrault V could support human life. Nearly every condition necessary for human colonization was in place, from temperature to gravity to distance from its star. The planet boasted an ample water supply and thriving plant ecosystem. While oxygen levels in its atmosphere were minimal, preliminary simulations had predicted successful terraforming over the course of only a few generations using comparatively simple breeding techniques. Discussions were already under way to send a crew to the planet that could bring back its native plant life, to splice the DNA the probes had found with that of native Terran vegetation. Aurora swore she would be a part of it.

For the next four years, she learned everything she could about space travel.

At age fourteen she did a science fair report on the launch of the first moon colonies. At fifteen, she aced 12th-grade physics. At graduation she walked across the stage to shake hands with her beaming science teacher amid the applause of proud parents. Next stop: MIT.

Two months later came the car crash. Dad had been crushed under an overturned roof. Mom died in the ER eight hours later. She grieved them, then pushed her grief to the side and kept studying. She convinced herself it was what they would've wanted.

Aurora was just finishing the first year of her undergraduate degree when NASA announced plans to construct the first manned interstellar spacecraft. The project would be helmed by the esteemed astrophysicist Dr. Pyotr Chekovsky, who had named the ship the *Spindle*. It was shaped like a gigantic wheel, rotating on an axis to simulate gravity in its rim, and driven by a long propulsion shaft that stretched behind the central hub, like a *Spindle* without thread. The vessel would bring seven astronauts and a handful of robot aides through the wormhole to land and survey the exoplanet beyond. Once there, they would spend a full Earth year collecting plant samples and conducting a series of experiments on Perrault V's surface before returning home. If all went well, the *Spindle* would emerge from the wormhole to a fleet of cryoships, ready to carry whole colonies of frozen humans (and the first crop of plant hybrids) to the virgin world.

Soon after finishing her degree, Aurora came onto the project as an astroengineer. As a graduate student, she'd been commissioned to design an elbow mechanism for a robot intended for use in the ship's construction. Several months later, an email confirmed her place at NASA, engineering landing gear for the *Spindle*'s suborbital craft, *Odyssey*. The job was a dream come true—the moment she saw the subject header, she grabbed her roommate from in front of the TV and danced her around their apartment for joy. It wasn't just a job with NASA; it was an opportunity to help contribute to the most ambitious step in space exploration to date. One that would soon be looking for a field engineer.

From the beginning, she gave the project everything she had. Every second in the laboratory was well-spent, as she pored over readouts and tinkered with blueprints to optimize the lander's design. She spent hours of overtime testing new ideas and running the simulation programs like an addict with a drug.

Sometimes the lab would receive a visit from a group of clean-shaven men with gray suits and lapel badges, scribbling down notes about her team's progress. Sometimes those clean-shaven men would interview team members about their performance. The rumour spread that they were looking for candidates for the ship's maiden crew. Aurora's heart skipped every time she saw one of them gesture in her direction. For anyone else, the pressure would have been crippling. Not for her. She wouldn't *let* it be.

She was getting on that ship.

It was two weeks into her work on the *Odyssey* that Aurora first met Phil. It was late, and she was hard at work on one of the lander's main gear actuators. Something was wrong with the computer simulation, and she wasn't willing to let the glitch sit untouched for an entire weekend. After a quick caffeine boost, she figured she'd be able to get the program working by midnight.

She ducked out of her office, keys in hand. Her footsteps echoed through long, empty hallways, clicking a steady beat across the linoleum. Presently, though, she heard another sound between her steps: a loud, deep, expressive voice singing at the far end of the hall. She recognized it: he (yes, definitely a he) was singing Aerosmith's "I Don't Wanna Miss a Thing". Aurora followed the sound through the maze of corridors to another office door, cracked ajar. The name plate read: "Chekovsky: Astrophysicist".

She was curious. She'd heard Pyotr Chekovsky speak in briefings and lectures before, and knew the voice serenading the empty halls couldn't be his. The graying physicist's voice, though strong, was that of an old man—far from the young, vibrant voice that echoed Steve Tyler across the abandoned building.

Aurora pushed the door open on the sight of a young man about her age spinning in his office chair, his fingers picking across an air guitar. He swivelled to face her and broke off from the music, a startled look frozen on his face.

Their eyes locked. Brown eyes, she noticed. Handsome features. A shock of auburn hair.

He flashed her a grin; embarrassed, playful. "Hi," he said perkily.

Aurora smiled back and tucked her hair behind her ear. Her stomach fluttered. Without breaking eye contact, his hand slipped over to his computer keyboard to the volume button. The 1990s-era crooning grew quieter.

"Most people use headphones," she said.

"Sorry. I'll keep it down."

"No, it's... it's fine. You sound good." She pointed to his name plate. "Chekovsky?"

"Phil Chekovsky, yeah."

"Related to Pyotr?"

"His son. And you are?"

"Aurora King. I'm in the astroengineering department."

"King?" he asked. "I've read some of your work. Your preliminary designs for the *Odyssey* landing gear are really impressive."

"Thanks," she said. She felt a swell of pride, and at the same time, wished her hair looked a bit neater. "Working late tonight?" she asked.

"Yeah. You headed home?"

"Actually, I was gonna go for a coffee run before settling in for another couple of hours." She hesitated. "You wanna come?"

"Sure," he said, grabbing his jacket. They made for the exit.

"So Aerosmith, huh?" Aurora remarked. "Old song."

"I like old songs," Phil shrugged. "I'm impressed you recognize it." He held the door as they left the building, then led her across the parking lot to his silver Toyota.

"My dad read me a lot of old sci-fi when I was a kid," she told him. "With all the wormholes and exoplanets showing up in the news, he wanted me to understand what it meant that the mythology of the past was becoming real in our lifetime. Read to me every night before bed— Herbert, Clarke, Heinlein. We watched a lot of old movies too. I saw the one the song was written for."

"That why you joined NASA?" he asked. "Science fiction with dad?"

"Something like that," she answered. Phil opened his passenger door, and she thanked him and ducked inside. He gunned the car's engine.

"I get it. When I was a teenager, I saw my dad looking over some of the data the probes sent back. He was bent over the table, pages open, morning sun streaming through the windows with Mom's pot roast still on the table. Cold from the night before. It was a big deal to him—how close we'd just gotten to actual interstellar expansion. It became a big deal to me too, I guess. All the more so now that we're about to launch the *Spindle*."

Aurora bit her lip. "I'm—I'm going to be on it."

"Really?" Phil pulled out of the parking lot. "Like, you've already been accepted for the crew? I thought that wasn't going to be finalized for another few years."

"No," Aurora corrected herself. "Not yet. But I'm determined. It's what I've been working toward ever since they announced the project."

"Isn't your dad gonna miss you?"

She hesitated. It wasn't something she liked talking about, especially with new people. She traced mental fingers over the throb of old grief.

"He died," she said at last. "Both my parents did. Car crash, years ago."

Phil braked to a halt at an oncoming stop sign. He looked across at her. "I'm sorry," he said. He was, too; she heard it in his voice, that sense of loss that so many people tried to fake when they heard her mention the crash. Not Phil. She could tell almost immediately—Phil wasn't fake.

"I know they're proud of me," she said. "My dad gave me this dream. My mom taught me I could reach it. I'm going to be on that ship."

"They sound like pretty great people," he said. "And honestly, you might make it. Like I said, I've read some of your work. Your parents have good reason to be proud." He checked the traffic and turned onto the street-lit road.

"Thanks," she said. "How about you? Would you join, if you had the chance?"

"Hey, if I apply, I won't need anyone else," Phil joked.

"Yeah?" Aurora raised a playful eyebrow. "You're going to pilot the ship through a wormhole, leave her in orbit, camp out alone on an alien planet for a year, run a series of complex atmospheric, botanical, and microbiological tests, adapting to any and all problems you find along the way, and then come back with the appropriate plant samples—by yourself?"

"Totally," he said.

Aurora chuckled.

"Honestly, I dunno yet if I want to ride the *Spindle*," he said, more serious now. "I probably could. I'd miss everyone back home, but my parents would be proud."

"But?"

Phil held his breath, deciding whether or not he should say any more. "I feel like a lot of people think I'm only here because my dad's in charge. I don't want to give them another reason to think that. Like I'm inheriting a kingdom or something."

"But you're not."

"I hope not. I wanna work for it. Just like anybody else."

"Okay," Aurora said. "So, you're not at NASA just because your dad got you a job. The project is clearly something you care about. If you were in my situation, you'd apply, right?"

He glanced across at her. "Definitely," he said. He checked his mirrors.

"So why?"

"Because it's the next big quest," he said. "The next leap forward in the human journey. Like we're looking for something, on orders from deep down in our collective gut. It's something... almost primal, I think. Like the first time somebody rubbed two stones together to make fire.

Or the day you moved out of the house because it was time to grow up."

Aurora nodded.

"And this isn't just your leap, or mine, but everyone's. Once a few of us do it, all of us can do it. You know what I mean?"

"Yeah," Aurora whispered. "Yeah I do." She nudged his elbow with hers. "I think you should go."

"Yeah?"

"Yeah. I'd fly a starship with you. Who cares what anyone else thinks?"

"Sounds like you want me to care what you think."

She rolled her eyes, but couldn't hide her smile.

He nudged her back. "Hey. Maybe I will," he said.

Questions and answers bounced back and forth between them ("What's the first thing you would do once you touch down on the planet's surface?" "What do you think will change the most on Earth during the voyage?" "If you could take one famous dead scientist to Perrault V, who would it be?"). Phil was smart, she found. Smarter than most of the guys she'd met in college. Funny. Confident. Inventive and curious. Any silence between them during that evening didn't last long.

Aurora was almost disappointed when they reached the drive-thru and put their conversation on hold while the speaker box took their order—and sighed, only half in frustration, when Phil insisted on paying for her coffee.

They returned to the research building, and a small, responsible part of Aurora thought that would be the end of it. She'd go back to her lab, he to his office, and both would have a productive evening. They reached her door, still talking, neither quite willing to part ways, until one or the other realized they'd been standing there for almost three hours. It was two-fourteen in the morning when Aurora drove home, her glitch still unsolved, remembering what Einstein had said to explain time dilation. "An hour sitting with a pretty girl on a park bench passes like a minute. That's relativity."

Phil asked her to dinner the following week.

By the end of that year, Phil had gotten his PhD, and both of them were candidates for the *Spindle*'s maiden crew. Aurora was ecstatic. The following

September, the project coordinators shipped Phil, Aurora, and the rest of the relevant personnel up to the *Sky Castle* space station for further trials and training. The selection process would conclude in orbit.

Aurora could still remember the day she'd first seen *Spindle* in her *Sky Castle* dock—almost-built, glimmering white in the sunlight, drifting out from Earth's shadow in the launch station's slow, graceful ballet-orbit around the planet. Technicians and construction droids hovered in and out of her shadowy edges like dragonflies over a pond, edging the proud vessel nearer and nearer completion. She hung on Phil's shoulder as he pointed down the *Spindle*'s propulsion shaft, where her lander blueprints had begun to take form. He wrapped his arm around her waist and pulled her close.

"See that?" he whispered to her. "That's *yours*."

Aurora and Phil met Malcolm Fairburn the day after their arrival. He was one of thirteen other candidates for the mission

—an astrophysicist, like Phil, who'd served as a critical consultant for military spacecraft. He had angled features, a patch of beard over his chin, and focused, iron-gray eyes that never missed an atom.

"Chekovsky?" he asked, on hearing Phil's name. "Like Pyotr?"

"He's my father."

No response.

Fairburn was smart. Solitary. He'd been working in space a few months longer than Aurora and Phil had, and his experience made him a prime candidate for the crew. But something about him irked her. His curt manner with the other contenders, maybe, or the way he studied her in the mess hall without a word.

Training on the *Sky Castle* was intensive. Space exploration had come a long way since the early years, but the candidates still needed to learn how to manoeuvre the craft. They logged hours together piloting space suits and operating maintenance equipment, running and repeating drills and tests for every situation they might encounter. The purpose was to give each of them a well-rounded practical fluency with all the ship's operations. Should anything happen to one of them, the others could still make it home.

Aurora noticed Fairburn's approach to the program early. He was competitive. Incisive. Any perceived mistake on the part of his fellow candidates, no matter how invisible to anyone else, and he'd slice into them like a scalpel—without anaesthetic. Actual *kindness* seemed out of his reach, like a skill he had never learned before.

Maybe no one's ever been around to teach him, Aurora thought.

Only she seemed exempt from Fairburn's snide remarks. Phil thought he knew why. "He's in love with you," he said, one night over dinner.

The words made Aurora cringe. While Fairburn's rage never settled on her as a target, there was something else in him that did; a silent, hungry attention that made her edge to Phil's other side every time she caught Fairburn staring at her in the dining hall.

Even Fairburn's attempts at friendliness, especially to Phil, were seasoned with a tone of subtle but unmistakable condescension. It was especially potent in the nickname he chose for him: "Prince." *So much for not inheriting a kingdom*, Aurora thought.

"He's projecting," another candidate, Dr. Basile, told Phil after a particularly tricky exercise.

"What do you mean?"

"He was working on a project for the military before this," Basile said. "Project Diablo. I heard his dad was the project director. I doubt he really *worked* his way up here."

Aurora wasn't sure. Fairburn might be an asshole, but he was also smart. And he wasn't the only other qualified candidate under consideration, either. Dr. Basile had applied as the crew's geologist. Dr. Kavita Tennyson was a veteran biologist who had been researching Perrault V fauna from the beginning. Dr. Percy Forrest had been a child prodigy, designing parts for the *Spindle* when he was seventeen years old. Aurora wasn't sure how she and Phil could compete. And if only one of them was destined to reach the new world, she knew that they couldn't remain a couple forever.

That was the problem with time dilation. Relativity. Time on the voyage would pass slower than time on Earth. The seven explorers who set out on the

Spindle would have to leave everything behind—their homes, their families, their whole lives—with little remaining on their return. Aurora's only living family was an estranged aunt living in Alaska—but her attachment to Phil wouldn't so easily dissolve. If she boarded the *Spindle* without him, or vice versa, their relationship couldn't last.

She'd tried to talk to him about it already, on Earth. Four times she'd screwed up her courage to do it. Twice she'd let the opportunity slip. The third time she'd gotten distracted; he'd cooked them dinner, stubbed his toe on a corner at his house, and spilled spaghetti sauce all over the floor. She'd laughed. He'd started a meatball fight. By the end of it all, they'd given up and ordered Chinese.

And the fourth time—well, the fourth time she'd asked him. Out loud. He'd changed the subject.

But Aurora was resolved to talk about it before the final roster was revealed.

Phil took her to the observatory tower the night before Director Walter was scheduled to make the final announcement. He'd brought two ration packets for dinner, and together they hovered in front of the bright-strewn glass dome, gazing out at the glittering promise of faraway starlight. Deep purple gas threaded its way across the porthole. Phil reached for her hand and wove his fingers into hers.

Please God, let them send us both.

"Hey, Phil?" she said.

"Yeah?"

"What happens,"—he cocked his head, waiting for her to continue— "tomorrow, I mean,"—her pulse quickened, screaming at her not to ask the question— "what happens if they only take one of us?"

The words hung heavy in the weightlessness.

"I hadn't thought about that," he said at last, with a theatrical nod. "I figured they'd just—*give* us the mission and tell everyone else to stay home."

"I'm being serious, Phil."

"So am I," he said. "I don't need six crewmates to make it through a wormhole and back." His fingers stretched, then tapped against her knuckles. "Just you."

She paused.

"What if I can't go? What if they send you and not me?"

Phil let go of her hand and rotated himself around her, his back to the glass. She stared up at him, meeting his dark eyes against the backdrop of the stars. He took her hands in his, and she felt him pull her up towards her, like gravity, like the beginning of a dance. His hands were warm.

"You're the youngest person in the running," he whispered, "and the smartest person on this station. You'll be the first one on the roster. Trust me."

"But what if—"

He shook his head. "No. No what ifs. No backups. Whether we're on one side of the wormhole or the other, you're the only crewmate I really need."

She nodded and smiled. *Man.* Those brown eyes.

Please, God.

He rotated again to look up through the inky veil of gaseous whorls to the stars on the other side. "One more night," he said. "And then we leap."

Aurora woke the next morning to find Phil already out of bed, clicking through his messages.

She unclipped from her berth, slid open the glass partition, and scrambled forward, desperate with anticipation. She touched her hand against his back and ran it up under his arm, wrapping him in a close hug. She inhaled deeply, stretched herself upward and glanced toward the screen from over his shoulder.

He spun around to face her, blocking her view of the monitor. He rolled his bottom lip back against the edge of his top teeth—Phil's telltale sign of disappointment.

"Did we make it?" she whispered.

When he didn't respond, she raised her eyebrows. "Come on. Don't joke about this."

His eyes darted around the compartment. Other candidates, bleary-eyed and slow, began to unclip from their berths. Fairburn glared at him as he emerged from behind his glass. Phil said nothing. His eyes began to water.

"Phil!" Aurora said, as she tried to push him away from the monitor. "Did we make it!" He reached behind himself and grabbed the underside of the keyboard in an effort to steady against her push. She pushed harder.

"Answer me or get out of the way, Philip Chekovsky. Are we on the *Spindle*?"

He shook his head and bowed low. "I'm sorry, Aurora," he whispered. He pushed up toward her, his arms outstretched in a comforting hug. She heard a catch in his throat. She shoved him away from the keyboard to look at the screen.

She scanned the opening paragraph and down to the list of names. Her mind barely registered most of them. But there, in professional black font, in a column with five others, were the names "Chekovsky" and "King."

Phil sputtered a mischievous giggle and floated to his berth. Aurora checked the list again, praying she wasn't dreaming. Andersen. Basile. Chekovsky. Grimm. Forrest. Tennyson. King.

They were going. *Together.*

Aurora turned to Phil and grinned, then shot toward him and pressed him against the bunks. They locked eyes, and she grabbed his arms to pull herself close.

"Hey," he said, grinning. She felt him poke at her stomach and looked down.

There was a small felt box in his hand, open.

"Will you marry me?"

A white diamond sparkling against the black. Like starlight.

"I kinda want to say no now," she said, smirking through the tears.

"Would you say yes if I got down on one knee?" He grabbed a handhold and tried to edge himself lower, fumbling an attempt to remain kneeling. He stared up at her, weightless.

She savoured the tension as long as she could, but in the end, couldn't stop the laughter. "Yes," she said. "Yes, I'll marry you."

He pulled his fist back in triumph, then pushed upward.

Aurora shot a playful blow to his abdomen. His torso crunched forward, and he gave an exaggerated *oof*.

"Don't do that again," she lilted. Whatever shock Phil had felt from the hit had vanished, replaced with a wide smile. She grinned as he pushed himself forward, and pulled her close, his hand on her back.

Then she kissed him.

The clock read 4:23 am. Three hours before wake-up call. Four before departure. Aurora unlocked the glass partition and pushed out from the berth. She hadn't slept.

She slipped on her jumpsuit and floated to the observation deck. The Earth spun beneath her, cities radiant in the shadowy blue.

Another planet. She was going. The most important journey in human history, and she would be a part of it.

And the *Spindle* was only the beginning. Once they made it back through the wormhole, the colony arks would be close to finished. Research into cryonics technology had already begun; the hope was that this would make it easier for the colonists to board their ships *en masse*, as well as conserve supply storage space on board. On reaching orbit, the colonists would remain frozen, then be thawed in waves as the settlements grew in population capacity. With any luck, in only a few decades after their arrival, Perrault V would have a thriving human colony on a breathable new world. For Aurora, the morning's launch would mark a new beginning for the human species—the dawn of the interstellar age.

And she and Phil were going to be a part of it. *Together.*

She admired the ring against the starlight.

A few hours and a wash later, she made her way to the dining hall for breakfast. Basile and Forrest greeted her as she gulped down her rations. Phil wasn't up yet. By 7:42 she still hadn't seen him—under half an hour before launch.

She drifted into their quarters and found him lying still in his berth. She tapped her fist against the glass.

"Phil."

No response. He looked sick.

"Phil!"

His eyes, half-opened, were rimmed with fatigue, and the rest of his skin was an inflamed red. At first Aurora thought it was the light in the berth—but no, after a closer look she could see something was wrong. She pushed toward the exit and saw someone blur past.

"Dr. Tennyson?" she called into the corridor. "I think something's wrong with Phil!"

Dr. Tennyson grabbed a handhold, turned, and floated into the sleeping quarters. She peered at the body beneath the glass.

"How long has he been like this?" she asked.

"He was fine last night."

"Anything he could've eaten? Any change in his schedule that might have let an infection into his system?"

Aurora shook her head. Her stomach turned with every question. The station's crew had been under rigorous hygiene standards since their arrival—Earth's germs were a far more serious threat in orbit, to say nothing of whatever microbes they might find in the alien star system— but there was no mistaking it. Phil was sick.

"You need to get to the medical bay," Dr. Tennyson said, pushing Aurora into the corridor.

"But Phil—"

"We'll take a look at him once we've got everyone under quarantine. We're going to have to push the launch back a few days at least, no stopping that now—but Director Walter will still want to limit the delays as much as possible. If we can figure out how the disease got into his system, we can still salvage the mission."

Aurora knew she was right. A deep space voyage would weaken the immune system and strengthen diseases in ways that could prove fatal if the dangers weren't addressed as quickly as possible. They couldn't afford unnecessary risks.

They notified Director Walter, and after a brief consultation with the medical crew, Aurora and the rest went into quarantine. Until they could be sure that no one else was contaminated, the *Spindle* project was on hold.

Aurora lay strapped against the infirmary bed, cringing under the medprobes and trying not to ask for news of the others. She knew the doctors were doing the best they could, but the suspense was growing unbearable. They'd come so close to beginning the journey, and now they faced a danger that could halt the whole project.

Phil. Where was Phil?

She tried to sleep, with little success. Another doctor came in to run more tests —blood scans, micro-x-rays, psych evals. She pressed him for updates, but got nothing. Finally he sent her to wait with the others. Silent stares haunted the room as they waited for the ordeal to end.

By morning they were free to move about the station. Phil's berth had been decontaminated, and he'd been transferred to a medical station for further diagnosis. The rest were given a clean bill of health. Director Walter met with them that evening to brief the remaining crew.

"Research into what happened is ongoing," the director told them grimly, "but we're confident the disease is contained." His attention bounced from one crew member to another. "What that means is that we're going ahead with the *Spindle* mission—but we're going to do it without Dr. Chekovsky."

Aurora's stomach knotted.

"We need an astrophysicist," Dr. Andersen pointed out. "We can't complete the mission without one."

"Dr. Malcolm Fairburn will serve as Dr. Chekovsky's replacement."

"There's no chance waiting for Phil to recover?" Aurora asked.

Walter shook his head. "It's still too early to know how long that would take," he said. "That's why we're sending Dr. Chekovsky Earthside to recover. But we can't afford to wait. If we do, the Earth's orbit will carry us away from the wormhole. It'll cost us precious time and resources."

Aurora wanted to hit something.

"I know you two were close," the director told her. "I'll give you until tomorrow."

"Phil?"

"Hey," he breathed. Even in her headset, he sounded different from the man who had proposed to her less than 48 hours ago. Weaker. Aurora's stomach turned.

From the communication tower, she could see the bright white of the medical station hovering over the tinted horizon, falling forward into the Earth's grim shadow. How had things gone from so right to so wrong in only two days?

"How are you feeling?" she asked.

"Pretty tired," he replied. "Doctor says my fever's at 103. Last few trips to the restroom have been kinda brutal. They're sending me home in a few hours."

Aurora nodded. "We're going ahead with the mission," she whispered.

The medical station began to fall past the sunset.

"I heard."

"We didn't decide what would happen. If one of us couldn't go."

"Didn't we?" Phil's voice cracked.

"You said you wanted me to be your crewmate," she whispered. "That whether we were on one side of a wormhole or the other, I was the only one you'd really need."

"Yeah," he said. "Yeah, I did." His voice gave way to silence—a burning, heavy silence, buffering the next painful word like the wall behind her buffered the fury of solar radiation.

"So now what?" she asked.

"Well," he said, "I think you get on that ship, and you bring us back some plants."

Aurora shook her head. "I can't."

"Can't what?"

"Can't leave a day after you asked me to marry you. I mean—I love you, Phil. I can't abandon you after that."

"You also can't pass up this opportunity."

The silence was uncomfortable.

"You need to get on board that ship, Aurora," he said. "I'll be here when you get back."

If only that were true, she thought. "I can't."

"Alright," Phil said. He took a deep breath. "Then, Dr. Aurora King,"—God, she loved how her name sounded on his tongue—"I'm breaking up with you."

She gave a bittersweet laugh.

"You're just no good for me," he continued. "You're smart, and beautiful, and *awesome*, and bound on a journey through a wormhole to an alien star system. And that's just not the kind of woman I can, in good conscience, tie down. So I'm leaving you."

"I'm leaving *you*," she said, wiping a tear from her smile.

"Hey, promise me this," Phil added. "Make sure you're the first to touch your foot to the new planet. And say something good."

"I love you, you know," she whispered. "I'll always love you. Make a girl really happy for me someday, okay?"

"I will," he said. "I love you too." The words sounded casual, like he was just leaving for a night and would see her again in the morning.

If only.

Aurora saw almost no one else until the pre-launch briefing nine hours later. She felt their eyes on her, heard the whispers when her back turned, and endured the silences that told her how little they felt they could say. She sat through the briefing, hardly listening to any of it, praying, instead, for one last chance that Phil might be well enough to go with them after all.

But the crew boarded the *Spindle*, and Aurora and the others watched from the observation deck as Commander Grimm unlocked the ship from her docking bay. The launch sequence blurred past in what seemed like minutes. She didn't try to savour it. All of the excitement she'd expected to feel as the *Spindle* broke away from *Sky Castle* seemed forced and insincere the moment they actually detached. How could any of it matter, without Phil on board beside her?

The crew slept in shifts. With no sun to distinguish between days, a preset twenty-four hour schedule served as its replacement. Aurora woke every cycle feeling sick, loss churning through her insides like machinery. Sometimes she wished it would end. Other times she dared not let it. It would feel like betrayal, letting her memory of Phil float out into the void. Like he hadn't really mattered to her. And no matter how much the loss of him hurt right now, she refused to admit that he had not mattered.

For most of the voyage, she cut herself off from the rest of the crew. Dr. Basile tried to keep them occupied as best he could—the man had an endless supply of games and anecdotes—but Aurora found it difficult to stay interested. She secluded herself for days in her quarters, combing through the selection of books and movies on the *Spindle*'s mainframe. Sometimes recorded a few video greetings to send home. No one ever replied. And in the silence between the stars, her grief howled.

The others worried. All of them had had some idea of what Phil had meant to her, and most had been there for the proposal. Dr. Tennyson noticed the ring around her neck, and tried talking to her about it once or twice. Aurora brushed it aside. As kind as the thought might be, Aurora was perfectly capable of doing her job without a breakup counselor. She could deal with loss, she insisted. She'd done it before.

Soon everyone's concerned looks gave way to indifference. She'd join them when she wanted to, they reasoned, but until then, pressing her was futile. Eventually most of them got used to her absence.

She wondered if Phil had gotten used to her absence.

It wasn't just grief that drove her further from contact with the others. It was Fairburn. The distance from Earth had increased his irritability. Whereas

Aurora kept to herself as often as possible, Fairburn hovered right on the edge of nearly every activity, silent—until he saw the opportunity to mock someone. His insults grew sharper, crueller, followed by deafening silences as everyone realized that shooting back would waste oxygen.

Once, at dinner, she heard him mutter something about moving on. "It's not like they were evenly matched, after all," he said. "*She* made the roster on merit."

Aurora couldn't take it any longer.

"You talk as if Phil were some third-rate hack who just lucked his way into his candidacy," she rejoined. "Like you think mocking him will make us forget the truth. But it won't. We all know you were second choice."

Fairburn glowered, and she knew she had struck a nerve. *Good*, she thought. She kept on. "And if you really have a problem with nepotism, I think it's time you looked in the mirror. Everybody knows how you got to be on the *Spindle*."

"And how was that?" He raised an eyebrow.

"Wasn't your dad the director of some military project?" she asked. "Project Diablo? Pretty easy to get a position like this when your father's willing to pull strings for you, I bet."

He paused. It was the first time she'd ever seen him hesitate in responding to someone. Then he smiled, a harsh, self-satisfied smile.

"Project Diablo was a disaster," he said. "It was a waste of precious time and manpower, and the military cut the funding for it early, on my advice. Since the director of the project resigned in disgrace, I don't see much point in asking favours from him." Not *my dad. The director.*

His glare, unbroken, forced her to retreat back to her dinner. But she went to bed that night thinking on it, and realized that at last she had found a chink in his armour. A weakness—one she wouldn't soon forget.

It wasn't until the *Spindle* reached the entry to the wormhole that Aurora began to take a real interest in the mission again. The call went out across the ship; Commander Grimm's firm German voice woke the few sleepers, and everyone filed into the command module. Aurora crowded in with the others, strapping in and grabbing a handhold on the far wall.

The wormhole gaped before them on the other side of the glass. Distant stars and gases warped along its rim like shadows on the ripples in a pond. Aurora felt a lump in her throat as she thought about what they were seeing. They were already farther away from Earth than any human being had ever been. And now, there it was: that sphere-shaped gravitational anomaly tunnelling through spacetime and across the observable universe. The one she had been chasing since grade school, the one she'd left behind everyone and everything to find. The crew tethered themselves into place as the ship arced around the tunnel, orbiting toward it in a long, silent fall.

"Hold on, everyone," Grimm said. "Here comes the drop."

The spatial shimmer began to twist and elongate like a rubber band. Aurora felt her stomach turn inside her. Her teeth clenched. She heard something rattle at the back of the module, something that she hoped was tied down. Another rattle. She felt vomit burn the back of her throat and prayed the ship would hold together.

She looked back to her fellow crew members. Fairburn's head was tipped upward, wide-eyed in a silent expression of terror. Basile held his head in his hands. Tennyson had gone unconscious. She wasn't sure how long this went on, but then, everything went still.

Aurora relaxed. Her stomach heaved, her head ached, but it was over.

"We made it," Grimm said.

Aurora breathed a sigh of relief as others whooped around her. She unstrapped herself and floated forward, hardly daring to believe it. They were through.

The *Spindle* entered orbit around Perrault V about two months later. The clouded white atmosphere veiled a world of virginal ocean blue, patched with continents of dark red deserts, snow-capped mountains, and blue-green forests stretching low and deep through waiting ravines.

Aurora made Grimm promise to put her on the first landing mission. If something went wrong with *Odyssey*, she argued, it would be good to have an expert aboard. Tennyson and Andersen went with her, while the other four remained in orbit.

Dr. Andersen winged the *Odyssey* lander toward a grassy clearing at the mouth of a river, near where the long-dead *Olive* probe had landed to conduct its atmospheric tests centuries before. The three women felt the landing gear unlock, then touch down gently on the alien turf. Aurora felt Tennyson's hand on her shoulder, and the biologist mouthed "Well done" under her helmet glass. The astroengineer smiled back. Then the boarding hatch opened with a slow *vvvvt*, and at last Aurora saw the alien world.

"This is for you, Phil," she whispered into her oxygen mask, though no one heard it on the official recording. It wasn't 'One small step for man,' of course, but she didn't care. There was a victory in that step, even if it felt bittersweet. A step violated for being taken in Phil's absence.

The ground was damp after heavy rain a few hours before, and glistening water droplets clung to the edges of tall blue-green grass. Her suit's readout confirmed the old probe's findings: the sliver of oxygen in the air was too sparse to breathe, but still detectable. *We'll change that*, Aurora thought. She inhaled deeply, and thought of what it would feel like to set foot outside on this planet without an oxygen tank on her back. *One day.*

The rest of the crew arrived several days later to set up camp. The planet was astonishingly well-suited to human life; its days were about eighteen hours long, its gravitational pull was comfortable, and there was a vast landscape to explore. Aurora and Basile spent the following weeks mapping the surrounding area, cataloguing plants and animals, taking soil samples, and testing the water supply. After a month, they traded the ship's rations for food native to the planet: large, egg-shaped fruits that tasted halfway between an apple and a peach. Dr. Tennyson took DNA samples from Perrault's vegetation, and spent days poring over the data in the lab. Fairburn spent the evenings in isolation.

Aurora was reading in her room one night, though, when his silhouette appeared in the doorway. She looked up from her book and swallowed.

"What do you need, Dr. Fairburn?"

He stepped inside. "Call me Malcolm."

"Why?"

"We don't have to go back with the plant samples," he said. His voice was hard. "The air filtration system in the habitat would provide enough oxygen for the two of us for a long time. After the others leave, we could wait here for the first cryoship." He walked further into the room and stood at the foot of the bed. "We —you and I, I mean—could give them something to find when they arrive."

A sense of unease crept into her at his words. "Something like what?"

"A colony."

Aurora was incredulous. "You're asking me to have your children?"

"With Chekovsky gone—"

"You took his place on the ship. That doesn't mean you have a right to take anything else."

"It wouldn't have worked out, you know. You and Phil. It never does."

"Get out, Fairburn."

Fairburn was silent, but didn't leave. Fine, then. If he wouldn't leave, she would make him. She knew by now what would make him uncomfortable.

"Is that why you boarded the *Spindle*?" she asked. "Something didn't work out? A breakup, maybe? Or a divorce. Or maybe you just realized that no one on Earth would miss you. And you don't know how to change that—so you tell other people that no one really cares about them either. For you, that's all there is left."

He bristled, but said nothing.

"Is that what your dad did to you?" she continued.

"My dad didn't do anything to me."

"Did he do anything *for* you?"

Fairburn glared.

"So he left," she guessed. "And you found him again. Or someone did, anyway. In charge of a flashy new experiment for the US military."

His silence told her it was true. For all his talk, Fairburn never denied the truth when someone else spoke it. Especially now. He couldn't.

"Beloved father and husband to a great big happy family," he finished.

"But not yours," she realized. There it was. Fairburn's wound. She eased up. "I'm sorry, Fairburn."

Fairburn didn't seem to notice her apology. "He was a decorated soldier who failed the only thing he was ever good at," he said. "Dismissed from his new post in weapons development because his own son tanked his idea. Because he was too proud to admit who I was. Even to his other family." There was contempt in those last two words.

"And now his own son's made history," Aurora finished. "In a way he never could. He can't claim credit for that without acknowledging who you are."

Fairburn nodded.

"I'm sorry he hurt you, Fairburn," she said at last. "But that doesn't change how I feel about Phil."

"Still?" Here, too, there was contempt. Bitterness.

"Still."

"Decades have passed on Earth. Even if he survived the typhoid, by now there's nothing left."

It was her turn, now, to feel the wound throb. Damn you, Fairburn. *Just when I start to feel sorry for you, you show me why I shouldn't.* "I thought I told you to get out," she said.

"Aurora—"

And then she realized.

"Who said it was typhoid?"

Fairburn looked like a deer in headlights. "The doctors—the medical personnel said—"

"No one said it was typhoid." Her feet slid off the bed and she stood, glaring. "We left before the final diagnosis."

Fairburn said nothing. She felt the old scar of Phil's absence bleeding anew, and the blood turned to venom in the silence. She stepped closer. "You bastard."

"We cured typhoid long ago, Aurora."

She cut him off with a cold slap.

Fairburn let out a trembling breath. "I didn't kill him."

"'Decades have passed'," Aurora spat. "'By now there's nothing left.' God, how did you even get the virus onto the station? You must've been planning it for ages, just in case you didn't get in."

"You won't tell," Fairburn said. "You can't prove anything—and our mission can't afford to lose a man if something goes wrong. You need me. They all do."

"Get out," she ordered, "and I won't tell anyone."

He glowered and obeyed.

Fairburn kept his distance in the weeks after she rejected his proposal. He had to. He knew, by now, how much she hated him; how nothing in the world would ever reverse what he had done. *Fine*, Aurora thought. *If that's what it takes.* Hatred was the language Fairburn understood best.

He tried to pretend it never happened. Avoid unnecessary contact. He knew she knew the truth, and that she would always know the truth. It was true that telling anyone right now would cause further division in the crew, and they might still need each other to return home safely, but once they did, she wouldn't need him anymore. If he wanted her to keep his secret once they arrived home, it was in his best interests to behave himself. Yes. That, at least, was a barrier Fairburn would respect.

But there was no healing in this. Knowing the truth, warding him off, didn't bring Phil back. She felt it all the more now, in fact. Phil was dead by now, probably; and if he wasn't, he would be before she got home. She thought of her parents all over again, the way she had wept at their funeral as they lowered the coffins into the ground. They'd been killed by a drunk driver. She'd seen a photo of him once online, and had felt sorrow for him, more than anger. He'd done a bad thing, but he probably hadn't woken up that morning with murder in his heart. But Fairburn had planned this. He'd *wanted* to take Phil from her.

She felt empty. Like the wormhole. After Phil's death at Fairburn's hand, that emptiness was the only thing left.

Little changed for Aurora in the final months on Perrault V. Dr. Basile kept taking soil samples. Dr. Tennyson continued her survey of the planet's greenery. By the end of their stay, they were confident the biology teams on Earth would be able to engineer a strain of Perraultian flora to terraform the planet's atmosphere. Their tenure on the planet ended, and at last, the seven explorers returned to the *Odyssey* lander, docked with the *Spindle*, and began the long trek home.

Aurora woke to a knock on the door of her quarters. It was Dr. Tennyson. Several hours had passed since contact with the *Sky Castle*, and she was here to announce their docking with the station. The ship had stopped spinning, and dozens of astronauts, scientists, and executives were waiting on the other side of the airlock, eager to hear the details of the voyage. Aurora dressed and followed her colleagues through the airlock, dizzied with new faces beaming smiles.

She was shipped to Earth with the rest of the crew and met with a triumphant welcome at NASA headquarters. The new director called a press conference, and ushered them down a hallway lined with photographs of directors past (Walter's and Pyotr Chekovsky's among them—Aurora noted the dates printed beneath each one with a twinge of grief) and into a room filled with shouting reporters, cameramen, and public sponsors, eager to learn all they could about Perrault V.

After the commotion had died away, one of Aurora's attendants tried to explain what had changed in her decades of absence. Private corporations had begun to expand their reach beyond the moon's orbit, and asteroid mining had made great strides in the construction of a colony fleet. The first ten colony arks were nearly ready, and they could expect to begin human migration in less than two years. Cryostasis had been successfully tested soon after her departure, and with the data the *Spindle* crew had gathered, everyone was enthusiastic that plant breeding could begin in the labs of the colony ships.

The *Spindle*'s crew spent weeks in a cycle of briefings, board meetings, and talk show appearances as people clamoured for insight on what was next. Aurora found it difficult to keep up. She found it difficult to even want to. Eventually she requested a year-long sabbatical. She needed distance from the busyness of the world. She would use her time off for research; to catch up on the various advances in astroengineering that had occurred since her departure. When the year was over, she could then resume her work preparing for mankind's next great leap.

Once the new director granted her request, Aurora bought a small home in Orlando and began her research. It was a welcome escape from all the media attention—and gave her something to do aside from thinking about Phil. After all, for all his cruelty, Fairburn had been right. Phil was long gone now.

One morning, though, Aurora heard a knock at her door.

"Dr. King?"

The woman was tall, with curly raven hair and mocha skin, dressed in a gray pantsuit and carrying a briefcase. There was something about her eyes that looked familiar—something Aurora at first couldn't quite identify.

"Yes?"

The woman offered her hand. "I'm Dr. Penelope Chekovsky," she said. "I'm a medical researcher at the University of Miami. It's an honour to meet you."

Aurora furrowed her brows. By now Phil, if he had still been alive, would be 108 years old. The middle-aged Penelope was too young to be a wife. "Like Philip Chek—"

"His niece," the researcher corrected her. "His younger brother Troy was my father."

"Oh," Aurora nodded. They shook hands. "Dr. Chekovsky, I don't know what they told you about me and Phil, but—"

"Everything," Penelope interrupted. "They told me everything. Your first date. Your work on board *Sky Castle*. The proposal. And the day after, when he got sick and you had to leave him behind." Her mouth curved upward in a kind smile. "You told him to make a girl really happy someday."

The memory of her own words stabbed.

"What I can do for you, Doctor?" Aurora said. Whatever else happened, she wasn't going to break down in front of a stranger at the front door.

"I'd actually like to do something for you, Dr. King," Penelope said. "There's something of Phil's that I'd like to show you." She nodded toward the ring, still hanging around her neck. "Is that the one he gave you?"

"With all due respect, ma'am, that was a long—"

"Please," Penelope insisted. "Do you still love him?"

Aurora didn't know what to say. It all flashed through her mind again: boarding the ship, crossing the wormhole, her first step onto the planet. The bitter night with Fairburn, and all the anger and confusion that had come after it. And then the return to dock with *Sky Castle*. It all felt so hollow. Marred by his absence. A full year of her life—the one she'd spent her life working for—and he hadn't been in it.

Did she still love him?

"Yes."

"Then come with me."

It was sunset when Penelope's SUV pulled in front of their destination a few miles out from Orlando: a wide gate in a high chain-linked fence with thorns of razor wire lining the top. The guard at the toll booth waved them through, and Penelope led Aurora into a lifeless gray building, with tinted windows and a handful of cars in the parking lot. Aurora followed, trying to understand what all of this had to do with Phil.

Penelope had refused to address her questions during the drive. "I'd rather show you than tell you, Dr. King," she'd answered.

They walked past the secretary and down a few labyrinthine hallways to an elevator waiting for their arrival. A black scanner stared from the wall, and Penelope pressed a key card to it.

The elevator began its descent. Penelope hummed a familiar tune under her breath, and Aurora strained to hear it. Gradually she recognized the melody. In a hundred years, she could never forget that song.

"Aerosmith?"

"I heard that was how you met."

Aurora nodded.

"You haven't asked about him," Penelope remarked. "Philip, I mean."

"Is that a question?"

"Yes."

"I meant what I said. I really did want him to move on. Continue his work. Fall in love." She paused. "I just didn't want to have to think about the man I loved—the man I *love*—wasting away over long years with someone else. I didn't want to think about him dying." She stared at her blurred reflection in the elevator door.

"We've cured typhoid, Dr. King."

"Can you cure time?"

"Maybe."

The elevator stopped and the doors slid open to a well-lit medical examination room. The place was set up with a heart rate monitor, defibrillator, hospital bed, refrigerator, and various other medical instruments. On the far side of the room lay a long box of padded gray, waist-height, topped with a long near-opaque white glass cover the length of a full-grown man. A circular light along the side glowed white, and along the floor a series of cables fed into the box's underside.

Aurora approached the box like a pilgrim approaching a shrine. The blurred outline of a face stared out at her from behind the glass. She drew her fingers over the surface. It was cold.

"Philip Chekovsky wasn't just an astrophysicist," Penelope said. "After his rejection from the *Spindle* mission, he went back to school. His work in cryonics is a big part of the reason the Perrault colonies are now possible."

Aurora looked to Penelope in awed disbelief. "You mean he's—"

Penelope nodded. "A little cold, maybe, but he's in there. He's been waiting for a long time." She pointed to a fingerprint scan beside the white light on the side of the cocoon. "It's coded to you. You want to wake him up?"

Aurora's heart quickened.

Alive.

Phil was alive. Dreaming. Right in front of her. A fingerprint scan away from waking up.

She pressed the scanner.

The bar of light rolled up and down the screen. There was a beep and then a click, and then the glass cover slid off the sarcophagus with a steamy hiss. She heard short gasps of breath spurting out from an ancient respiratory system.

Aurora peered inside.

Dark brown eyes looked up at her and blinked. Squint. Blink.

"Phil?"

She touched her palm to his frozen cheek. Breath steamed from his mouth, warm to her touch compared to the cold of his skin. A hand reached up and grabbed the edge of the coffin. Phil pulled himself upward, shivering, his face still caked with ice. He wiped his hand across his eyes and stared at her. Another blink.

"Aurora?"

The voice. His voice. The one she'd heard echoing Aerosmith lyrics through the halls of the research building so many years ago. God, she'd missed that voice, the one that should have filled all the silences she'd travelled since their call before the launch. Aurora grinned and wrapped his frigid hand in hers. For all the weakness his body had endured during cryosleep, she felt the strength in those fingers as they closed between her own.

"You're alive," she breathed.

The icy Phil nodded. "I promised you I'd make a girl really happy someday."

She kissed him, and it was as if all the years that had stood between them melted away in that kiss. He was here. Here, and alive, and young, and *hers*. Her lips remembered the taste of his, eager and lively even under the cracks that had formed in frozen years. She smiled between each caress of his mouth with a delight far greater than she had ever expected to feel again. His kiss woke something in her, and promised it would never again have to sleep.

"I love you," she gasped between kisses. "I'll always love you."

"Always," he replied.

Finally they pulled away. Phil staggered to his feet. Penelope found him a blanket, and together they checked his vitals. Fifteen minutes later he sat on the hospital bed, eating a ration packet.

"What was it like?" he said. "Perrault V, I mean."

"Do you want to see it?"

"Go there?" Phil asked. "With you?" He reached behind her hair to unclasp the ring from around her neck.

She nodded, moving her hair out of the way. "They're projecting only five years before the first colony ships launch," she told him. "You ready to make the leap with the rest of the human race?"

"Yeah," he said, smiling. He took her hand and slipped the ring back onto her finger. "I mean... I've got the only crewmate I'll ever need."

See J.A. Legg's story "Till All the Hundred
Summers Pass" online at Metaphorosis.
If you liked it, leave a comment. Authors love
that!
Remember to subscribe to our e-mail updates so
you'll know when new stories are posted.

About the story

One of my favourite things about being a story
audience is when a story comes to a crisis point that
goes one or two ways, and realizing to myself, "This
next part could go a number of different ways, and I
don't know which one it's going to be, but I'm certain
I'm going to enjoy it." Of course, every writer has to
commit to a direction (or end the story and let you
wonder for yourself what happened next), and that
gives the rest of us the opportunity to imagine the
alternate ending. That's how "Summers" began for
me; I took a popular rendition of a classic fairy tale and
privately wondered what would've happened if the
tale had gone another way. The science-fiction setting
came later, and with it, a resolution that brought the
twist back to its roots.

A question for the author

Q: What inspires you?

A: Other people, mostly. I'd be a fool not to recognize how much I am indebted to the genius of those who came before me—from famous storytellers I may never meet to the family and friends that have helped me sharpen my skills along the way. Somebody once said all art is theft, and if I ever try to disagree with them, I'll be on pretty shaky ground.

About the author

Jordan Legg is originally from Oshawa, Ontario, and holds a degree in English and Creative Writing from the University of Windsor. He is an amateur cyclist and sketch artist, as well as an avid reader and writer of speculative fiction. He currently teaches literature and history to preteens and teenagers at a private school in South Asia, where he's lived for several years.

@TheJordanLegg

A Seedling in the Dark

Eleanor R. Wood

He pined for the sky first. It was a constant he had always taken for granted, even when stargazing on crisp winter nights with his dad. But he soon missed the ground more. The cool scent of earth, the lush green of grass and clover that concealed an entire world of wonders. He'd spent countless hours on his belly in the meadow, watching beetles and ants and grasshoppers going about their lives in their towering forest home. Spindly harvest spiders, ladybirds, and snails. He missed them all with a terrible yearning. The toads would be spawning in the pond about now, long threads of jellied beads left in the wake of their orgies, to be collected and grown into tadpoles on windowsill jars.

He wondered if he would ever see a tadpole again.

"When can I go outside?" he'd asked his mum on the third day.

She had taken his hand and looked into his eyes.

"Darling, we can't go outside. Not for a long, long time."

"But why? There haven't been any explosions for days!"

"We've been through this, Jeremy. The explosions have filled the air with germs. It will be too dangerous for years. We're safe down here. But we have to stay here until it's safe up there."

"But what about all the animals? Won't the germs make them poorly?"

"I don't know, love. But nature always finds a way, you know that."

She hadn't answered any more of his questions, and he'd sat on the sofa in the tiny living area thinking about them on his own while she warmed tinned pasta for dinner.

As the long days crawled past, he began to realise how caged bears felt at the zoo. All their pacing, with no trees to rub against or leaf mould to dig through for grubs. He wanted dead leaves under his feet, and trees to look for birds' nests in, and badger setts to wait outside until it got dark and they woke up and nosed their way into the world.

He'd tried to pretend he was a badger and the bunker was his sett, but it was no good. Setts had tunnels that led to fresh air and forest and sky. The bunker had a door that led to a metal ladder that led to another door, sealed and bolted and windowless. He wasn't even allowed outside the first door, never mind that one.

"Why don't you play a board game with Charlotte?" Dad interrupted his misery.

"I'm fed up with board games." It had been weeks. They'd played every game in the bunker half a dozen times.

"Don't be daft — you love them. Come on, I'll play too. What d'you fancy?"

"I don't care." He knew he was sulking, but he didn't care about that either.

"All right, we'll let Charlotte choose." He called her in from the bedroom Jeremy and Charlotte shared. It had barely enough room for two beds and David's cage.

Charlotte chose Hungry Hungry Hippos, which was stupid and noisy and nothing like real hippos. Jeremy played anyway, because there was nothing else to do and he kept imagining the toads trying to spawn but dying from the germs instead, and it made him feel like the whole world was ending and nothing would ever be alive and free again. He and his hippo gobbled up dozens of plastic marbles until Mum said it was time to get ready for bed.

He put fresh water in David's bowl and covered his cage with its night-time cloth. The cockatiel chirped at him and settled down. To David, the world was exactly the same as always, only with a different view. Jeremy envied him.

They did school around the dining table every day. Sometimes David was allowed to perch on Jeremy's shoulder. Charlotte was learning her numbers and letters. Jeremy was learning about volcanoes. There was a chapter on fossils coming up and he couldn't wait to get to that.

"If all the animals die, will they turn into fossils?" he asked Dad.

"I expect some of them will, but it takes an awfully long time."

"I know. Hundreds of thousands of years." But still, the idea of a paleontologist in the future finding fossilised mice and stoats and blackbirds made him feel a little better about their probable deaths. Maybe they'd draw impressions of blackbirds with scarlet plumage or mice with long fur.

It had been three months since they'd all been bundled down the metal stairs. Three months since Dad sealed the top door with a hiss. Three months since Jeremy had seen a beetle or a spider at the centre of her intricate web. But at least he'd seen a living bird every day. He'd had David to feed, and clean out, and draw in intricate coloured-pencil lines. And now even that was gone. Jeremy had found him on the bottom of his cage, cold and stiff. He'd been off his seed for a few days, but there was no vet down here in the ground and all they could do was keep him warm and hope he perked up.

But he didn't. He died. Jeremy had held his soft little body for hours, refusing Mum and Dad's attempts at gently prising him away. He had cried until his throat was dry, and touched every inch of David's soft grey feathers, the white ones on his folded wings, the bright yellow down on his head with its vivid orange cheek spots. He'd stroked David's delicate crest, forever flattened now, and his curved seed-eater's beak and tiny branch-gripping claws. He mourned his friend, his bird, and with him, all the other birds he would never see. He grieved for the last non-human in his life, and hated, with a ferocity he had never experienced, the people who had dropped the bombs.

When he finally relinquished David's body to his dad's care, he curled up on Mum's lap and sobbed anew.

"Oh love, I'm so sorry." She had tears in her voice too. "I know how much he meant to you."

"How will I ever be a naturalist now, Mum?" His breath snagged on a sob. "What if I never see another animal?"

"Of course you will. One day, we'll all climb out of here and greet the world, and you'll see animals and birds and insects again."

"But how?" His anger flared. "They're all dead! Everything is dead except us!

What if David was the last bird in the whole world?"

She had tried to soothe him with more words, but he barely heard her over his weeping. The scope was too great. The sadness was too immense. He wanted to walk in the woods more desperately than he had ever wanted anything in his life.

They had art class with Dad once a week. Everything in the bunker was precious, but Dad had provided enough art supplies. They had to use both sides of the paper and all their pencil shavings went into the composter, but there were plenty of watercolours, and Jeremy was painting David from memory again.

"Beautiful shadowing, Jer!" Dad peered over Jeremy's shoulder.

"Thanks, Dad." Jeremy admired his painting. "Do you think I could make a model of him? A lifesized one?"

"What, like a sculpture?" Jeremy heard the approval in Dad's voice. "Now that'd be an excellent project for our next lesson."

Jeremy smiled. "Yeah. A sculpture."

"Fancy that, Charlotte?" Dad asked.

"Like playdough?"

"I'm sure we can get playdough in on the action." Dad winked at her.

They spent the next week finding sculpting materials. Recycling was the bunker's foremost rule, so anything discarded was fair game.

Jeremy's first David sculpture was a wire coathanger frame coated in papier-mâché. It wasn't very good; the frame was wonky and its head was out of proportion. But Jeremy curled its wire feet to the perch in David's cage even so, covering it over at night as if it were inhabited by David's chirpy soul.

Looking for new materials became Jeremy's obsession. He was allowed to experiment with heating old tins into malleable form. He cut a plastic tub into interlocking shapes like a balsa model. Mum got very cross when he unravelled one of his jumpers to wind around a new wire frame. He heard them talking about it in the kitchenette one evening.

"This can't carry on, Craig," Mum said. "Everything we brought down here is precious. We need to repurpose all of it if we're going to make it out of this."

"I know that," Dad said. "But just look at him, Heather. He hasn't been this content since we left home. I can't see anything more worthwhile than directing his energy."

"We need to survive for at least five years to be sure this thing's died out. We didn't bring sculpture materials into our calculations."

"We didn't bring our nature-obsessed son into our calculations either. You've seen how he's been. I'm afraid it's going to break his spirit, being stuck down here without so much as a blade of grass. Maybe... maybe it's time to show him."

There was silence. "You know how I feel about that," Mum said at last.

"We put it there for a reason." Dad's voice was soft.

"Yes. And that wasn't to give our son false hope."

Jeremy had no idea what they were talking about, and if he dared ask, they'd know he'd been listening. So he boxed up his curiosity and shelved it at the back of his mind. For now.

He was allowed to continue making sculptures, but only with materials he was given. He made models of David until he'd perfected a cockatiel. His aluminium body was almost the right shade of grey and his head was the perfect size, painted dandelion yellow with bright orange cheeks and a soft crest of brushed yarn. His talons could be bent around a perch, or flattened to stand on a table, or tucked into Jeremy's jumper so the bird could sit on his shoulder.

He'd been so proud.

"That is fantastic, Jer," Dad said. "From the corner of my eye, I'd think that was really David on your shoulder."

He wasn't really David, though. He didn't chirp, or turn his head on one side and whistle the way Jeremy had taught him. His body was cold metal instead of soft down, and if anything, he made Jeremy even sadder that David was gone.

He awoke one night from a dream he couldn't remember, a dream filled with loss and grief. He was sobbing before he was fully awake. His whole body ached with it. He curled on one side and wept, wanting Mum and Dad but unable to get up and go to them. His David sculpture perched on his bedside table, silent and pretend, and he just wanted to see a real bird again, just one, flying or nesting or singing in a treetop. His head throbbed, his pillow was sodden, his body was racked with it.

And then Dad was there, gathering Jeremy in his arms, holding him tight, Mum just behind, reaching a hand to his back.

"It's a dream, Jer, it's just a dream, mate. You're safe. You're all right." Dad rocked him in strong arms and soaked up Jeremy's tears with his nightshirt.

"I wish it... was... a dream," Jeremy hiccuped. "But it's not. We're really down here, and I can't go outside ever again."

Charlotte was awake now, and she was crying too. Mum went to her. She and Dad looked at each other across the cramped room.

"All right," Mum said. "You can show him."

"Show me... what?" Jeremy's breath hitched as he tried to stop the flow of tears.

"Come with me," Dad said, and took his hand.

He'd always thought it was just a cupboard, housing pipes and electrics and boring things not worth investigating. And it did have those things... but behind them, at the back, there was a ladder of metal rungs protruding from the wall.

"Up you go," Dad said, right behind him.

He climbed, still shaky from crying. At the top of the ladder was a square platform, just big enough for two people to sit side-by-side. The ceiling was only a few feet high, so Dad had to crouch low to squash into the space.

And set into the ceiling was a skylight.

"The sky..." Jeremy craned his neck to peer up at the blackness. It was cloudy, but there was a moon.

"There it is," Dad said, pulling Jeremy close so they could look together. The oblong of sky was small, but the spill of moonlight was enough to illuminate the space where they sat.

"Why is this here?" Jeremy asked. "Why didn't you tell me about it?"

Dad inhaled slowly. "Well, it was supposed to be at the centre of the bunker, so we'd have some natural light. But Mum worried it might make things harder for us, being able to see out to the world when we couldn't be in it. And I thought maybe she was right about that. So I changed the layout plan and built a cupboard around it, so it was still there without being a constant reminder of what we were missing. We didn't tell you because... we thought it might make you sadder than you already were. But I've never seen anyone as sad as you were tonight, so we realised maybe it could help you feel better."

The realisations were dawning on Jeremy. "I'll be able to see what the weather's like! And look at stars... and..." *What if a bird flies over,* was his thought, but he didn't voice it because there might not be any birds and he didn't want to feel sad again.

"Can I, Dad? Can I come up here sometimes?"

Dad kissed the top of his head. "Yeah. If it makes you feel better, of course you can."

At first, he went up every morning before breakfast, to check the weather and report to his family. Charlotte came up a few times, but she soon got bored with the view.

"You can't see anything," she complained. "Just the sky and nothing else!"

"Don't come up here, then," Jeremy said, defensive of his patch of sky.

He started going up the ladder whenever he missed the outdoors. Just looking at a piece of the outside world soothed him and made him feel connected to it again. One evening, he and Dad piled blankets and pillows on the platform and stargazed, watching pieces of constellations glide in and out of view until Jeremy fell asleep. He woke up there alone the next morning, sunlight on his face.

"You let me sleep up there," he said to Dad at breakfast.

Dad dolloped porridge for him. "I didn't have the heart to move you."

"Can I sleep there again tonight?"

Mum and Dad looked at each other. "I'm not sure that's sensible," Mum said.

"Please?"

"Yeah, can he, Mum?" Charlotte piped up. "I liked having my own room."

Dad laughed and gave Mum a helpless shrug. Mum sighed. "All right. But if it starts making you feel upset, you come back to your bedroom. Okay?"

"Yes!" It was half agreement, half joy. He hadn't felt upset at all since Dad had shown him the skylight.

The platform became his new bedroom. The skylight was his own private window.

He would fall asleep looking at the stars and wake up amongst a shaft of sunlight or a patter of rain on the thick Perspex. He was still confined, but the outdoors was there, right there, and contentment began to nudge at the empty places in his soul.

It had been a year since they stumbled underground and closed the world off. A year of cramped space and brittle emotion. A year without the breeze on their faces or new grass between their toes. A year without a single insect or stream minnow or trill of birdsong.

Jeremy's hours of gazing through the skylight had shown him that Earth still turned on its axis, that the Moon still accompanied them on their journey through space, that the seasons still brought rain and sun and snow that hid the sky until a thaw. He'd watched grass grow at the edges of his view, reaching tall and turning to seed and then dying back again. He'd seen leaves scutter across the skylight and frost form branching patterns and clouds of all varieties.

But he'd seen no signs of animal life.

He hoped that his view's limited scope simply meant he was missing them as they bypassed the bunker. That he'd never been looking at the exact moment a bird flew over or an insect buzzed past. But as time went on, he had to acknowledge the germ-filled air must have harmed them. That they just weren't there anymore. It broke his heart, but he didn't dare share it in case his parents made him return to his bedroom.

He watched David Attenborough documentaries until he could recite the narration by heart. He learned about the nitrogen cycle and copied pictures of leaves from his tree guidebook. He fell asleep every night with his face turned to the skylight and imagined the world full of animals, happy and thriving with no people around.

And then, one morning, a snail was there.

His breath caught in his chest as he woke to find himself looking up at it sliding slowly across the skylight, oblivious to the racing heart and burgeoning joy its passage caused in the human four feet below. Its trail glistened in the morning light as its suctioned foot propelled it across Jeremy's window to the world. He stood and pressed his face as close as possible, palms flat against the skylight, drinking in the sight of a living creature, willing it to slow down so he wouldn't have to watch it leave. He moved with it, his nose separated by inches of Perspex. As it glided over the side of the skylight, back to dew-damp grass and whatever hollow it sought for its daily rest, Jeremy felt his heart simultaneously squeeze and lift. He hated to see it depart, but the wonder and beauty of it made him soar.

His first proof that things still lived outside the bunker. That all creatures hadn't been killed. He leapt down the ladder and yelled his newfound truth.

"A snail! Mum, Dad, I saw a snail! Everything isn't dead, it's not! There was a snail on the skylight!"

Mum looked up from laying the breakfast table. Dad stopped stirring the porridge.

"That's fantastic, love." Mum smiled at the grin on his face.

"If animals are alive, it must be safe now!"

"Not necessarily, mate." Dad's tone was cautious. "It's great news, but one snail doesn't make it safe for us."

"But... maybe it's the beginning of it being safe," Jeremy said. "If a snail's alive, other things must be too!"

"Jeremy..." Mum put a bowl of porridge in front of him. "I'm delighted you saw a snail, but it's not evidence that other animals are alive, or that we could be. You don't even know it was healthy. Now eat your breakfast."

Even the monotony of porridge couldn't dampen his spirits. "But it looked healthy! And there can't just be *one snail*. Ecosystems don't work like that. There have to be other things living out there."

"*Jeremy.*" Mum raised her voice. "Eat. Your. Breakfast."

He swallowed a lump in his throat. He thought they'd be as excited as he was.

"It's great, Jer," Dad said. "It is. But you mustn't let it get your hopes up."

Jeremy looked down and ate his porridge in silence.

"I wish *I* could see a snail," Charlotte said wistfully.

Dad was an engineer. Mum was a mathematician. What did *they* know about nature? Jeremy knew lifeforms couldn't exist on their own. He just needed more proof, and then they'd listen to him and maybe realise there was no need to stay stuck down here. It could be his first Great Discovery: that the poisoned world wasn't poison any more. He didn't tell them; he knew if Mum sensed this new fixation, she'd ban him from the skylight. He couldn't conceive of losing his only link to nature. He'd shrivel up and die like a seedling denied the sun.

So he lay under the skylight every spare moment, feigning tiredness or headaches or interest in a new book. He gave up television; why watch recordings of living things when there were real ones he might miss while his attention was on a dead screen? His snail didn't return. He watched clouds scudding past, stared at pattering rain, witnessed the pastel reflections of a dozen sunsets, but no sign of what he longed for.

Patience was something every naturalist had to cultivate. You could sit in a bog for hours waiting for a sighting of that rare frog, or train your binoculars on a single tree for days to witness chicks fledging, or stare at a skylight for weeks to catch a glimpse of proof that nature fought on despite the worst of humanity's follies.

When it finally came, he thought he'd imagined it. A flicker of movement, high and tiny at the periphery of his rectangle of sky. He blinked and stared. The light was fading and he'd been about to call it a day. His mind was playing tricks on him.

Again — that fluttering glimpse. And... another! Dipping back and forth, the erratic, flitting flight pattern that could never be mistaken for a bird. Jeremy felt the grin spread across his face even as tears pricked his eyes.

Bats. There were bats in the sky.

He gazed upwards and watched them dash back and forth across his foot-wide field of vision. He was laughing and crying at once, overwhelmed with joy at the sight of little mammals hunting for their supper.

As the light dissipated, he lost sight of them, but he lay there for a long time, high on relief and delight.

Hunting bats. That meant there were insects. He'd witnessed the top and bottom of the food chain. Predator and prey. An ecosystem supporting itself. Life went on outside the bunker. Animal life.

Plant life. It all had to be there, thriving and well. Everything wasn't dead.

Everything was all right out there.

He climbed down the ladder on trembling legs and ran to his family, who were huddled together watching an old movie.

"Mum... Dad," he began, trying to curb his excitement so he could calmly present his discovery. They looked up at him.

"I just saw bats." It gushed out of him. "Bats! Above the skylight, hunting insects!"

Dad smiled. "Wow. That's fantastic!"

"Wonderful, love," Mum said.

"I mean... they were hunting. That means there're insects, which means there's all kinds of life. They didn't all die!"

His parents glanced at each other. "That's really excellent news," Dad said. "Maybe tomorrow we can all look out and see them."

"Yeah! But..." They weren't getting it. "It must be safe now. If they're all right, it must be safe for us too."

"Jeremy, we've been through this." He could sense Mum trying to remain calm. "Seeing creatures outside is wonderful, but it doesn't mean the air is safe. Biological agents last for a very long time."

"There's a whole ecosystem out there, Mum!" His own calm was fleeing and he was powerless to hold onto it. "I know there is! And if they're thriving, why wouldn't we?"

Dad stood up and put his arms around Jeremy.

Jeremy shrugged away. "You're not listening!"

"No, *you're* not listening," Mum said. "The only way we're going to get through this is if we all accept the facts. The bacteria might not harm animals, but they *will* harm us. We all want to get out of here, Jeremy. We all miss nature. But it is *not safe*. It won't be for a long time. And I think..." She closed her eyes and took a deep breath. "I think it's time to go back to your bedroom."

Dad made a pleading gesture.

"No, Craig. Enough is enough. This isn't doing any of us any good. No more skylight."

"No! No, no, you can't!" The lurch in Jeremy's chest propelled him forward. "Mum, please! I won't look for any more wildlife, I promise!"

"Enough, Jeremy! I've had enough. We all have." She went to the cupboard and up the ladder. Jeremy tried to follow, but

Dad held him back with a firm but gentle arm around his chest.

"I'm sorry, mate. Mum's right. We need to be together to get through this. You can't keep living half out there, breaking your heart and ours."

"No, Dad..." he sobbed. "Please, I need it."

Dad just held him tightly while Mum dragged his bedding and notebooks and David sculpture out of the cupboard and into Charlotte's bedroom.

"Why does he have to come back in here?" his sister whined, following her mother.

"Because he does, Charlotte."

Dad bent his head to Jeremy's and hugged him. The tears drenched Jeremy's face.

He stayed in bed for the first two days. He didn't eat. He couldn't bear the thought of being shut back in this underground box with no windows. Especially now he knew there was wildlife out there. Charlotte sulked about having him back in 'her' room. Mum and Dad had hushed arguments, and Jeremy knew some of them were about the skylight. When he emerged, finally, with a touch of appetite, everyone tried to pretend nothing had happened.

"Macaroni cheese for dinner!" Dad said, mixing a packet of cheese sauce. Jeremy missed real cheese.

He glanced at the cupboard. He'd had half a plan to sneak up to the skylight after Mum and Dad had gone to bed, but he'd known they wouldn't make it that easy. The cupboard door was padlocked. He turned away and ate half a plate of macaroni before going back to bed.

Dad tried to interest him in art projects. Mum read aloud to him. Even Charlotte tried to cheer him up with board games and terrible knock-knock jokes.

But he didn't care about any of it. Nothing mattered any more.

Anger slowly replaced his sadness, and with it came a flash of rebellion he'd never imagined. He lay awake one night and hatched a foolish plan. He knew it was foolish and he didn't care. He just wanted to show them they couldn't keep him from nature. The cupboard door was locked, but Jeremy knew where Dad hid his keys. The secret nook was inside a kitchen cabinet, behind tins of beans.

He'd unlock the cupboard, barricade it from the other side, return to his skylight, and there'd be nothing they could do about it. He'd even sneak a stash of food from the pantry. He knew it was an unsustainable protest, but what could they do? They'd already taken away the only thing he cared about. There weren't any punishments worse than that.

He lay still and listened. The bunker was silent. Mum and Dad had gone to bed; Charlotte's soft breathing told him she was asleep. He tiptoed into the kitchenette. In the dim nightlight glow, he retrieved the keys from their hidden nook, grasping them so they wouldn't jangle. There were only a few on the keyring... there weren't many doors in the bunker.

The padlock key was the smallest. He was on the verge of sliding it into the lock when it dawned on him what he was holding.

One of these keys opened the main door. The door which led to the ladder which led to the outside door which led to the world. He wondered why the existence of this key had never occurred to him. He knew which one it was: it was bigger than the others.

He looked at the door, ten paces away beside the kitchenette. The door he'd only been through once.

You can't.

But he could. All he had to do was open it.

And then what?

Then he'd be able to climb up to the outside door. There was a lever to unseal it. He could go outside. Come back before anyone woke up. He could prove to them that they were wrong, that nothing would happen to them if they came out. Whatever they said, humans *were* animals. And animals were surviving out there. The bats and the snail were his proof. He would be theirs.

He'd made up his mind before he even realised it, before his conscience could protest again. He was at the main door, all thoughts of the skylight forgotten, and the big key slid in smoothly and turned with a soft click, as though the lock had been waiting all this time for him to open it.

He glanced over his shoulder, afraid someone had heard. But the bunker slept on. He opened the door.

The dusky light barely illuminated the short passage and steep steps. But he didn't dare leave the inner door open in case Mum or Dad got up. Later, he'd tell them he'd been outside, and they could all reunite with nature. But now was just for him. He was a few steps away from the outdoors, from fresh air and wild things, for the first time in a year and a half. He didn't fear it. He knew he wouldn't drop dead from bacteria. If they'd seen the bats, they'd know that too.

The cramped stairwell was pitch dark with the inner door shut. He found the railing and groped his way up. The only patch of light came from a keypad beside the top door. His heart sank. He couldn't just pull the lever and go out.

ENTER YOUR FOUR-DIGIT CODE, the display read.

What would Dad use as a code? He thought for a moment, then keyed in his own birth year.

It bleeped its acceptance and a mechanism clunked.

Jeremy grinned. *Too obvious, Dad.*

His heart rate increased as he pulled the lever downwards, releasing the door's seal with a soft hiss. He pushed it open and stepped outside.

His eyes closed in bliss at the cool night air against his skin, sweeter than anything he'd ever breathed. Tears squeezed under his eyelids and he laughed out loud as he lifted his head to the sky and spread his arms wide. *Outside, I'm outside!*

The relief overwhelmed him. He fell to his knees in the long grass, clutching the fronds and relishing their smooth stems against his skin and the rich scent of the soil beneath, and the ground, cool and firm and uneven and holding him up as it rooted him back to where he belonged.

When he lifted his head, it was later than he'd realised; dawn was glowing on the horizon. He stood and walked through the tall grass, leaving the bunker behind without a backward glance. The breeze caressed his skin, stirring the trees to whisper their greetings. He reached the steadfast boulder at the edge of the field. Its surface was rough and cool against his palm, and lichen tickled his fingertips. The landscape stretched away here, open and green, all the way to the distant city. He climbed the boulder and waited for the sun.

A blackbird began to sing. A thrill ran up his back at that sweet melody, the purest sound in nature. He drank in the song like a parched boy at a stream, and felt it restore him. *Birds. Birds are alive.* A robin joined in, and a song thrush, and the dawn chorus rose up around him like a devotion, welcoming the day, welcoming him back.

He watched the sky pale and turn to flame until the land was bathed in sun and at last he beheld what the bombs had done.

The once-ploughed fields were a sea of meadow grasses. His house, perched alongside, had been consumed by the Virginia creeper his mother had continually pruned. The lawn was a jungle, the fence was woven with ivy, and saplings grew in the driveway's cracks. The first bees of the day began their work amongst the wildflowers, and house martins dipped and dove in the air.

Bombs had sent people into hiding, and nature had rejoiced.

Far off on the horizon, where once spires had risen and sunlight glinted on glass, there was an indistinct mass of broken things and a ring of scorched earth. Yet even amongst the burnt wreckage, he could see hints of green at this epicentre of human disaster.

His parents had been wrong. Life was thriving stronger than ever out here. His heart exploded with it.

He had no notion of time passing as he revelled in creatures living and flowers opening. And then, from behind him, Dad's voice.

"Jeremy... what have you done?"

Disappointment, grief, despair... his father's tone reflected nothing of the joy in Jeremy's soul. He turned to see him walking through the grass, his pale face lined with hurt.

"Dad..." He smiled. "Look! It's safe out here! I told you it was."

"No, Jeremy, no, no, it's not." There were tears in Dad's eyes. "There are deadly germs out here. We told you that."

"But — look at the wildlife!"

Dad's arms dropped at his sides. "You don't understand, Jer. And it's our fault. We should have explained it to you properly. Wildlife is here, yes... and it's glorious. But humans can't be. No one knew if the biological agent would harm other species. It's wonderful that they don't appear to be affected. But for people, everything out here is contaminated."

Jeremy's protests died in his throat. He couldn't believe it. But Dad's face... he looked lost. Broken. Tendrils of fear crept around Jeremy's heart.

"Then... we have to go back inside?" he asked.

Dad clenched his jaw. "No. We can't go back inside. We're contaminated too now, you and me."

Jeremy noticed a pair of rucksacks on the ground outside the bunker.

"We can't go back in without putting Mum and Charlotte in danger. They mustn't be exposed."

"But... they can't stay down there on their own!"

"They have to. And the two of us... we have to get moving. Our best chance is to get as far from the biological radius as possible. If we're lucky, and if there are any doctors still alive who've figured out treatments, we might be okay."

The foundation of Jeremy's world buckled under him. "No, we can't leave them, Dad!"

Dad pressed thumb and forefinger to his eyes to push away tears. "We don't have a choice, mate."

Jeremy slid down off the boulder and ran towards the door he'd been so desperate to exit. Dad caught him with one arm and reeled him in tight.

"Let me go... I need to tell Mum I'm sorry!"

"You can't. You can't. They have to stay safe."

"Why did you come out, then? Why, if it's dangerous?" He twisted to face Dad.

"For you. I came out for you, Jer."

Jeremy felt the weight of his mistake like a mountain about to crush him.

"And now we need to go."

Dad went to the rucksacks and shouldered one. He handed the other to Jeremy. Poking out of the top was his David sculpture. Jeremy stared at it, numb and bewildered.

Dad stopped beside the skylight. Jeremy's window was just a strange hump in the grass from out here. Dad beckoned to him, seemingly unable to speak. Jeremy came reluctantly and looked down, into his haven... the tiny space that had instilled in him so much hope.

Mum and Charlotte's faces looked up at him, tears in both their eyes. Mum reached a hand to the Perspex and Jeremy knelt, sobs erupting from nowhere, and pressed his face to the skylight, still inches from theirs. *I love you,* Mum mouthed to both of them. Charlotte clung to her, weeping.

Dad inhaled a ragged breath and tugged Jeremy's shoulder. "Come on. We've got to move."

Jeremy peeled himself away, sick with regret. Dad was already on his way to the lane beside the house, wiping his face on one sleeve. Jeremy watched him for a moment, frozen, and then took David from his rucksack. He stroked the soft crest and then placed the memento of his beloved bird in the grass beside the bunker door. To stand guard? As grave marker for his first loss? He didn't know. But this David was of the bunker, as Jeremy was of the outdoors, and their ways had parted.

"Dad... wait!" Jeremy called as he turned away from David. Everything was happening too fast. He didn't have time to make sense of the upheaval he'd caused.

Dad turned back to him. It hurt Jeremy to look at his face. "What? Jeremy, we need to leave. Right now."

Jeremy fought the tears that kept trying to flood out of him. "Can't we just... stay at the house? At least be near Mum and Charlotte?"

Dad closed his eyes and took a long, slow breath. "You know we can't do that. And you know why."

"But I've been out here for ages and I'm not ill!"

"We don't know that."

"But —"

"*No.* No more 'buts'. No more 'maybes'. We all heard the bombs, we know how close they were, we know they brought deadly disease. We have to find help, Jeremy, if there's any help out there to find."

"Are you cross with me?" He didn't mean it to come out in such a tiny, sad voice.

Dad sighed, wearier than Jeremy had ever seen him. "There wouldn't be any point in that, would there?" He reached out his arm.

Jeremy ran to him and clutched him hard.

"Come on." Dad's voice was softer now. He rubbed Jeremy's back. "The sooner we're away, the better our chances."

Jeremy wiped his eyes and held onto his dad's hand like a little boy.

They left the bunker. They left the house. They began their long walk, and Jeremy knew, as his dad knew, that it might not save them. The long-rotted bodies they passed, in cars, in front gardens, were proof of the danger Jeremy had exposed them to. He squeezed his eyes shut at these confirmations of death's brutal reign.

But despite his loss, his fear, their terrible uncertainty, Jeremy's heart was soothed. For the hedgerows they passed were wild and teeming with life, and birds sang their summer songs of fertility and survival.

See Eleanor R. Wood's story "A Seedling in the Dark" online at Metaphorosis.
If you liked it, leave a comment. Authors love that!
Remember to subscribe to our e-mail updates so you'll know when new stories are posted.

About the story

This story arose from several sources, but its overriding inspiration was British naturalist Chris Packham's astonishing autobiography, *Fingers in the Sparkle Jar*. In it, he describes his early passion for nature - not only his childhood obsession with the natural world, but the deep solace and sense of belonging he found there, particularly as a boy who didn't fit in anywhere else. Around the time I read this book, I'd been toying with the notion of writing a story set in a survivalist bunker, and suddenly I was struck with the concept of a child who was deeply connected to nature and then cut off from it entirely. What would that do to a kid like this? What would it have done to Chris Packham as a boy? What would it do to me...?

I've also loved and thrived on nature since childhood, and the idea of being completely severed from it terrifies me. Being amongst nature is being surrounded by life. Being amongst non-human lifeforms takes our gaze away from ourselves and reminds us that this planet is host to far more than just human beings. In the story, Jeremy's desperate need to have that affirmed overrides every other concern in his imprisoned life, and ultimately takes him to a place of both tremendous joy and bewildering sorrow.

A question for the author

Q: Where do you write?

A: I write at my desk, in a room full of books and plants, both of which I find infinitely inspiring. My writing room has two large windows, so it's full of natural light, and there's normally at least one dog relaxing nearby. The desk is usually cluttered with hand-scrawled notes, as I vastly prefer writing story notes by hand, and although it may look chaotic to the untrained eye, I always know exactly where everything is.

About the author

Eleanor R. Wood writes speculative fiction and eats liquorice from the south coast of England, where she lives with her husband, two marvellous dogs, and enough tropical fish tanks to charge an entry fee.

creativepanoply.wordpress.com, @erwrites

The Nocturnals V

Mariah Montoya

In a world where each day and night lasts thirty years, Joah, Misla, and Damien have traveled into the Eternal Night to make contact with the humanoid creatures who live there—the Nocturnals, a people they used to fear. Now that they know the Nocturnals' terrible secret, they must warn their nomadic community of a planned massacre lying ahead.

To get back to sunset in time, Joah and the others travel deep underground to find fuel for Queen Usai's ancient starship. Deadly traps, a prisoner's betrayal, and a mysterious Leather Skin lurking underground threaten to tear them apart, but through it all, the three must persevere.

It's time to return to daylight. It's time to tell the Sunsetters the truth about the Nocturnals. It's time to destroy the real darkness once and for all, before the sun leaves them behind forever.

Part 5

Someone was knocking on Aoif Deckler's door.

He ignored the noise, staring out his window at the mountainous shadows darkening the valley where he had forced his people to settle. He could smell the salt from here. Just beyond those cliffs, the sun was balancing on the edge of a great sea, a sea he had been yearning to taste again ever since his boots had crunched back on brittle sand fifty-eight years ago.

"General Deckler, sir," a voice called from behind the door. "Please."

He tried to ignore the wretched knocking, but his captain's voice whined through the wood incessantly. After a few more ticks from his wristwatch, Deckler withdrew his feet from his polished desk and slammed them to the frayed, thin carpet.

"Okay, fine, don't piss off," he boomed. "Why don't you come in, then, Lincoln? We can have ourselves a little tea party while we're at it. Act like princesses."

The door burst open. Captain Lincoln stood panting in his doorway, the hallway behind him strangely distorted—its walls had been dented during their most recent Move. A silver badge gleamed on his chest, his hair shined with gel, and his hands were naked of calluses.

"It's a woman from the Dirt Slums, General," Lincoln breathed. "She's going mad down in the office. Tearing her hair out, practically. Won't stop screaming that she wants to see you, and well..." Captain Lincoln massaged his lotioned hands together. "You sent most of our security ahead with the first wave. We don't have any jailhouses. Or handcuffs."

No, Deckler had not wanted the officers and retrievers to come running when the Nocturnals—or rather, the Nocturnal *slaves*—invaded the Dirt Slums. He had sent those individuals ahead to camp out with the scavengers and sailors on the edge of the Green Sea, where they'd be safe.

Captain Lincoln, on the other hand, would probably get snatched up in his haste to help the chosen victims. So would the Dirt Slummer apparently banging around his office downstairs.

"What's her name?" Deckler asked the captain, his eyes flicking open.

"Lupita Fertheli, General."

The name stirred something vaguely familiar in Deckler's chest. Ah, he needed a cigar. His fingers twitched toward his cabinet, where his last roll of tobacco lay tucked away—but no. When they sailed the sea and left this piece of the aro behind, he'd only get one smoke. Better to save it for something more disturbing, more frightening, than a piss-poor bitch of the slums.

Deckler grinned, opened his desk drawer, and popped a candy into his mouth. He rolled the thing from cheek to cheek until he felt his teeth turn blue.

"Send her up, Lincoln. Let's see what she has to say."

The captain bowed and scurried away, his footsteps clunking down the portable stairs past the bend in the hallway. Moments later, a door from below banged open. Lupita Fertheli's shrieks crashed into Deckler's office moments before the woman herself did.

"I can walk by *myself*, thank you very much."

Lupita yanked her elbow from Captain Lincoln's grasp, took one look at Deckler lounging in his office chair, and slammed the door behind her with a violent kick of her fraying sandal.

"Well, good evening," Deckler said, half-amused, half-irritated. "Or should I say good night?" He glanced out the window, where the cliffs cast pools of darkness. He imagined he could see the outlines of the ships Captain Lincoln's men had built on the shoreline.

"It *isn't* a good night," snarled Lupita Fertheli. Her hair stuck wildly in every direction, witch-like. The palms she slapped on Deckler's desk left grimy handprints on a stack of papers. Hatred and fury bandaged the grief lining her face. "My son is still missing."

"Is he, now?"

The gears clicked into place. *Yes.* This was the woman whose son Joah Cadshaw had been trying to find for the law enforcement office. Deckler himself had halted the investigation so he could send

Cadshaw to do more important things, like getting the hell out of his way.

Judging by the repugnance pinching Lupita Fertheli's face, she already knew this.

"Where's Detective Cadshaw, General?" she asked now. Deckler felt a thrill of relief at the wobble infecting her voice. It wouldn't take long for the tears to flow, and when they did, she'd no longer seem to tower over him like a wiry-haired fortress.

"Cadshaw?" he asked, blinking up at her politely.

"Yes, *Cadshaw*. The one looking for my son. The one you sent away. I *know* he went to you after the Moving bells rang early. I *know* he left the community with another retriever. But I'm begging you—*begging* you..." And there it was: a glistening eye. "Tell me where Cadshaw is now," she said. "Has he found my Damien? Did h-he ever come b-back?"

"Listen, Lupita. It's Lupita, isn't it?" Deckler didn't wait for her to nod; he put a hand on the same wrinkled elbow she had yanked from Captain Lincoln. "I sent Joah out west to see if your son had... strayed. To see if he'd gone after the Nocturnals."

This was a lie, but when Lupita's shoulders sagged from their previous rigidity, he didn't regret it. He massaged her elbow, and she let him, sniffing up tears that wobbled on the edge of her nose. Such an *easy* lie. The truth hit harder, especially since he'd actually liked Cadshaw.

"But he didn't come back when I told him to, Lupita. Last I heard, he and Retriever Crane warned the grahsm miners about the early bells and continued west. The oil scavengers said they never saw them. As far as I know, Cadshaw's still searching for your son."

Or being hacked to pieces, he didn't add when Lupita split into sobs. He had his own suspicions about the fate of Joah Cadshaw: the man's enemy, the one who'd cut off his wife's head, hadn't returned from his western duties either. Just *poof.* Gone. Deckler had chuckled a little to think that the two would meet again when he'd sent Joah that direction, but now that neither had returned, it wasn't hard to imagine a bloody battle in the woods at sunset.

Ah, well. There were more important things. Like ships. Or the invasion that would tear through the valley within the next arcsec. Or the sobbing wench before him.

"Listen, Lupita, if you have an arcsec to spare, I could have my secretary make you some tea. Our herbalists found a new kind of mint on the way here, I'm sure it would help calm you."

He didn't know what made him say it. Why should he care for a grubby life like hers? The sooner she left his office, the sooner he could focus on his impending date with the Nocturnal king. But something in her wild, crazed face mirrored the smut of that horrible season after his mother's death and before he became general. When he had been poor and hungry and scared too.

Lupita Fertheli wrenched her elbow away from his stroking thumb, her eyebrows hardening. For a mad moment, she looked the same shade of sick Deckler's own mother had been so long ago. Flames pierced her eyes, and she thrust her chin in the air.

"I won't stay here if you don't have answers. I'm missing my *son*, dammit, and if you don't know what happened to Detective Cadshaw, I'll find someone who does."

She whipped around. Deckler's eyes followed her trembling figure to the door.

"Suit yourself," he said somberly, after one of those sandals had kicked it shut again.

He waited for the night to begin with tightly pressed fingertips. Nobody disturbed him again. He opened his drawer, popped more candy in his mouth, rolled it along his gums. The clock ticked. The shadows deepened. Eventually, Deckler hoisted himself up and approached the cabinet. He glanced at the glossy poster hanging above it, that many-eyed figure leering at him behind lamination. The image cheered him up. It was funny, really... he'd spent the last sixty years teaching his students at the Retrieving Institute that the creature painted on the poster was a Nocturnal: as far from the truth as day was to night.

With a whistle, he opened the cabinet door.

When the clock struck three degrees, smoke was already curling toward Deckler's ceiling. It was not quite nighttime, but the cliffs blocking the sun bathed them in a rich darkness. He strode to his window and thrust it open, inhaling that smell of salt and ocean breeze.

From the crevices in the distant cliffs, disfigured shadows scuttled into the valley. They wended their way between wheeled structures, into the slums that had Moved from *there* to *here*.

When the first screams rent the air, Deckler looked back at his pinned poster and winked at it, as if enjoying a silent joke with an old friend.

Joah watched the ground shrink through frosted windows.

As they rose above the netted treetops, the landscape became a mass of intersecting light. Patches of foliage were re-growing where their sun counterparts had died. Blades and leaves and trees glowed with the energy their roots had sucked from the ground. The plants were feeding off the reservoir of sunsap they had collected during the thirty-year day.

That same sunsap now fueled Joah's flight through the clouds.

As the clouds thickened, mist swathed his view of the aro below. He withdrew from the window and turned to find Prince Kal explaining various parts of the starship to a wide-eyed Damien Fertheli:

there was the control system, slathered in buttons and knobs more complex than any vehicle Joah had ever seen; and over *there* were the storage bins, metal compartments filled with canned sugar water, spare spider silk cloaks, and weapons.

I can take you up to see the generator, if you'd like, Kal told the boy.

Even after spending a whole season with the Nocturnals, Joah still marveled at the words hissing, not from the prince's lips, but from his mind. Telepathy suited the circumstance, though. It was hard to hear voices over the rattling of the starship as they flew.

Oh, yes, please, Damien said, obviously trying not to appear too eager. His face remained nonchalant, but his thoughts quivered with excitement. *I mean, why not?*

This way, then.

Prince Kal pulled a lever dangling from the ceiling. A narrow ladder unfolded itself from the upper floor, and Kal mounted it, motioning for Damien to follow.

When he and the boy had disappeared into the crawlspace above, Joah turned to Misla, who was fingering the rough wooden edges of the table quivering in the middle of the room.

"Are you alright?" he asked, touching the other end of the table. His mind mimicked his tongue, so he knew she'd be able to hear him as clearly is if he were whispering into her ear.

She had bathed since they had retrieved the sunsap from underground. Her hair fell in tight waves below her breasts, and she wore a honied blue dress made from one of the queen Nocturnal's old cloaks. A bruise spiraled around her neck where the creatural roots had strangled her below the aro. Beneath her dress, she wore another scar, the remnants of an abuser now gone.

Joah moved closer. She gave a hesitant smile.

"I feel sick, to be honest."

"Couldn't have anything to do with the fact that we're zooming through the air faster than the sun moves across the sky, could it?" Joah asked.

Her lips twitched.

"Could be. Or maybe it's because I'm about to confront the general I swore an oath to and tell him his ass is fried if he doesn't step down. *That* would make anyone want to puke."

"Hey, you know that's not part of the plan."

No, Deckler would never step down. They all knew that, even Damien. Their plan was no longer to fly to the Sunsetters and dissuade their general from a deed he'd been planning for six decades. They were heading southeast, yes, but toward King Isce's fortress instead, where they would kill the Nocturnal king before he could give his orders. If they made it in time, that was. And if they *could* kill him.

"Don't," said Misla, clasping her stomach. "I really *might* puke."

Again, Joah felt that desire to hold her, or be held by her, or do more than stare at her with a table between them. But he swallowed his thoughts and said, "Why don't you go to bed, then? If Prince Kal is right about how fast this thing flies, we'll be there in a dozen arcsecs."

"Yeah, okay."

Swaying a little, she crossed the circular room and approached one of the rounded outlines by the control panel. She pressed her cold palm against it. The wall slid upward obediently, revealing one of the tiny sleeping compartments Prince Kal had shown them earlier.

She paused outside the door, jolting as the starship rocked violently.

Will you come with me, Detective Cadshaw?

Joah's heart raged inside him, louder and more fearsome than Moving bells could ever be. He clutched the table's edge, more to steady his mind than his body. Outside, rain began to thrash against the glass, and the mist flared with occasional bursts of light.

I mean, why not? he said in the same offhand tone that Damien had expressed.

She rolled her eyes and ducked her way into the compartment, which housed a pull-down cot beneath some overhanging shelves. She crawled onto the mattress, sinking into its spongy material. Joah followed. He could hear the faint drone of Prince Kal and Damien's thoughts in the crawlspace above, but when he lowered the compartment door behind him, the buzz of their conversation faded. The only sound in here, it seemed, was Misla breathing.

He sank onto the bed, reaching out to find her in the denseness of this new, rich darkness. His hand found her shoulder; his fingers traced her neck, hovered over the bruise, and worked their way up to her chin, her lips. Hot desire shuddered through him, as if he'd inhaled sunsap.

She grabbed the back of his neck and pulled him onto her, and then their lips brushed against each other, and her thighs were wrapping around his waist, drawing him closer.

I want you, they said together. Their thoughts were merging, twisting and twining like the glowing designs of the aro during the Eternal Night. And they were kissing—he was tasting her, and she smelled like sweetened sunshine. *Misla, Misla, Misla.* He pulled up her dress, and…

In the darkness, it might have been Blair, the corpse of his dead wife lying in his bed, running fingers through his hair, muttering that she wanted a baby…

And Misla's thoughts scampered with panic too. In the darkness, it might have been Hickory, the corpse of her ex-lover bowing over her with that greedy stench of rape wafting from his tongue, ready to sink rotting teeth into the burn scar he had inflicted upon her…

They broke apart, gasping for breath.

No! Joah cried.

No, no, no, Misla moaned.

Tears scorched Joah's cheeks as he rolled away. He had thought he was over his wife, that he'd come to accept her death. And God, he really *did* love Misla. But his body shook with tremors from that morbid vision, and he knew he had *not* healed, had not yet reached the light at the end of his vast and monstrous tunnel.

Neither have I, Misla said. She was crying too, her breath hiccupping as their mingled tears dampened the pillows. She still felt haunted by her own personal chasm of darkness too.

"What do we do?" Joah whispered out loud.

They found each other's hands as the walls gave a nasty jolt.

"We help each other find the light," Misla said.

He nodded, turned toward her, wrapped his arms around her waist and buried his face in her neck. Yes, they would help each other find the light. He closed his eyes.

They'd walk the tunnel together, even if it felt like that walk would never end.

When they finally shot from the clouds, sunset pierced them through the windows.

Joah, Misla, and Damien squinted, shielding their eyes with their hands. Prince Kal donned his hood and clipped the edges of his cloak together, skulking in the shadows.

I can't touch the control panel anymore, the Nocturnal said, nodding at the stream of thin, orange light running from the windowpane to the many knobs and buttons. *One of you will need to follow my instructions to land. We're almost there.*

"I'll do it," Damien said.

Joah and Misla glanced at each other, but the boy had pinched his eyebrows together in obvious determination. With a unified nod, they stationed themselves on either side of him, ready to pounce on the panel if he ever became overwhelmed.

Okay, see that gear shift in the upper left corner? Yes, that's the one. Put it in low.

Damien did as Prince Kal commanded, his forehead wrinkled with concentration. He pulled levers, pressed knobs, and tapped keys with nimble hands. Soon they were plunging into a maze of cliffs and valleys and winding rivulets.

"Look," Misla said with a half-laugh, pointing, "I think it's that river we were going to float. The one that ran by the grahsm cavern. See how it's heading southeast."

Sure enough, a widespread snake of water glittered between canyons, and it led to—

"Oh," Joah breathed.

The horizon expanded as they descended, winking with pink light. And the sun—that brilliant bowl of orange Joah had so missed—teetered on the edge of a sea he had only ever heard stories about. It was, he thought as he stared out the window, like an upside-down sky, filled with rippled green water and sprinkled with stars. The fabled Green Sea.

Hard left, Prince Kal said. *We don't want to land on my father's front lawn.*

Damien drove the starship into a gulch surrounded by walls of rock. With Prince Kal's thoughts puppeteering his bony arms, the boy landed the contraption beside a twisting stream, where bushes and scrubs throttled its pebbled bank.

Now go, Prince Kal said, sinking into a crouch against the wall. *I can't go too near the castle, or my father might sense me.*

This stream leads straight to his fortress. And remember... They turned to look at him as they gathered their packs and rods. His eyes were mere violet slits within the darkness of his hood. *You may find it difficult to remember both languages without a Nocturnal by your side. Don't let yourself get disoriented. Find your tongue.*

A cold chill spread through Joah's abdomen at this newest thought. Of course. He had become so accustomed to using telepathy and his tongue, both with ease, that he had forgotten how Damien had described the Nocturnal language away from the Nocturnals: *"It's like somebody's calling your name through the far end of a tunnel."*

"Hopefully we'll find King Isce right away, then," Joah said grimly.

The star's double doors slid upward, steaming. Joah, Misla, and Damien clambered onto the rocks below, leaving the prince behind. The stream gurgled to their right, but they couldn't see past the tangled shrubbery congesting its bank.

"We'll follow the sound," Misla said, hitching her pack higher up her back. Joah adjusted his too and nodded. Inside their many hand-stitched pockets were packets of seeds, water cans, ropes of fibermud, and cloaks. But they clutched the most important tagalongs in their hands as they started down the narrow channel of pebbles between shrubbery and cliff: rods with darts coated in sunsap that they would shoot at King Isce when they encountered him.

The gulley twisted this way and that, narrowing and widening, sometimes speared with orange light, other times bathed in twilight shadows. As they trudged forward, the greenery thickened, and mud squelched beneath their shoes. They began ducking beneath gnarled branches, pushing through the thorny arms of bushes, clambering over moss-cloaked boulders in their path.

The foliage clotted like a shield. Spikes poked from stems, some the size of Joah's thumb, others needle-like and hairy, reminding him all too well of the Leather Skin living within the depths of the sunsap. Hickory's ax would have suited them well now, but they had left it lying in the water in the underground tunnel along with the broken shards of ceramic.

"C'mon, let's take the stream," Misla muttered.

They pushed their way to the bank and splashed into piercingly cold, glass-clear water, which rose up to Joah's knees. After a few arcsecs of following the current, their hands rigid around their rods, Damien whispered, "What's that smell?"

The stream had spread out like melting butter. The air tasted like salt and moss and something undeniably slimy. But it was fresh too, and Joah inhaled deeply.

"I think it's the Green Sea. We should be—"

They rounded a corner and stumbled to a stop, squinting at the sudden slap of naked sunset. The gulley had opened to a coastline spreading eternally in either direction. The stream itself joined an immense, lazy body of water up ahead, which met the sea with the tenderness of a long-lost lover's kiss. Soaring birds dotted the sky above the harbor.

And to their left, a vast, interconnected collection of turrets and towers lined the coast. This was King Isce's fortress, where the Nocturnal, his subjects, and his slaves Stayed.

"Okay, Kal said the cellar looks like a half-moon," Misla said, pointing.

One of the towers up ahead, separated from the rest, curved like a stone horseshoe. This was how Prince Kal had told them to enter the fortress. The cellar would lead to the kitchens, which would help them bypass any guards that might be standing by the front doors.

Joah nodded. They stooped low and trudged through the stream until it meandered right. Then they clambered onto the muddy grass and dashed toward that half-moon tower.

Joah's ears pounded with the impending crash of the sea. He didn't want to face King Isce. More than that, though, he didn't want to witness what lay inside that cellar. They had *planned* to gather any remaining human bones to bring back to the community. Proof of Deckler's treachery. Of their looming doom. But as they neared the cellar, Joah's heart sunk with a tingling suspicion that perhaps they were too late. Perhaps the invasion had already begun.

Okay, who wants to do the honors? he asked, his tongue too dry to speak aloud.

They had scurried into the cellar's shadows. Vines crawled up the stone, smothering the outline of those circular doors lining the curve of walls. One door stood naked, though, the vines around it snapped in pieces, as if someone—or something—had already pushed its brute way inside. Joah's head buzzed. He tried to expel his thoughts, but they resounded differently inside his ears. Weaker.

I'll do it, Damien said.

The boy was about to push his cold palm against the door when movement on either side of them made him flinch back. Two shapes emerged from the deepest thickness of vines: shelled bodies, hairy legs, imprints on their faces like many-eyed insects.

The Leather Skins stared at them. They didn't say anything, but Joah could hear the faint drone of their thoughts anyhow, like frantic voices behind closed doors.

The deed was done. It was too late. They, the Leather Skins, had been forced into the invasion, had hauled masses of bodies to this cellar. Their buggy eyes seemed to be bleeding a sour green pus, as if they had been hurt in the process.

Joah's head buzzed and buzzed, but he managed to say, *Get out of here, all of you. We're going to get rid of him. Head north. You'll find some ships. Steal one. Sail your way back to daytime.* He swallowed thickly, choking on tears. They could afford for the Leather Skins to steal a ship because the Dirt Slummers had already been taken. *We won't be far behind.*

For a moment, he thought they were going to close their pincers around his throat. But with a ticking, clicking sound, they withdrew hesitantly, then scuttled lopsidedly away.

Damien slapped the door in his haste to get inside, where his mother's body would no doubt be lying among bones. The door obeyed, grinding upward until a mouth-shaped hole opened in the stone before them.

Joah had a split second to process the heated, stifled darkness inside. Bodies stirred within the cellar's black abyss. There came the sound of grinding bones, clattering rocks, and clinking chains. Damien sucked in a breath, and Misla reached out an uncertain palm...

Then someone screamed.

Before Joah could back away, a hand emerged from the darkness within and jerked him inside. He hollered, twisting blindly. He felt his rod wrenched from his grip. Misla and Damien shouted beside him. The door behind them lowered with a resolute *thunk*.

"What are you *doing*? You can't let them see us," growled a horribly familiar voice. It was gravelly and gruff, and it belonged to the person now clutching

Joah's shoulder, forcing him deeper into the belly of the cellar. "To the honest depths of hell, I can't believe it. Detective Cadshaw and Retriever Crane. I thought you two were dead. And this little boy must be—"

"Damien!" a woman shrieked.

The buzzing in Joah's head swelled. He clamped hands over his ears, and realized, too late, that his pack was gone. He felt, rather than saw, a woman tear from the mass of huddled bodies surrounding them. He heard Damien cry out and cling to his mother, reunited at last.

But his mind couldn't comprehend what was happening, and Misla's own confusion met his like a tentacle of thought groping for land, for something to cling to in this darkness.

Why was General Aoif Deckler in the cellar with the very people he had handed over?

Why were the people—the living, breathing people—here at all? Joah had been prepared for the stink of rotting bodies, not for the stench of sweat and piss.

What are you doing, Deckler? he tried to rasp, but he couldn't find his tongue.

His foot lurched forward, kicking something small and hard on the floor. At the same time, the people around him began murmuring, and Deckler boomed, "I appreciate you trying to save us, retrievers, but we have a plan. You could have been *seen*, sneaking in like that."

What are you talking about? Joah tried to ask, but once again, his lips couldn't move.

Deckler seemed to hear him, though, and it was this, more than anything else, that spread ribbons of fear throughout Joah's body. He was immobilized, caught between two languages, but *Deckler* knew how to execute both perfectly. *Deckler* was still playing his game.

"If they see us trying to escape, we have no chance," the general said, his voice carrying throughout the cellar. Lupita muffled her sobs against Damien's hair. "But when they come in *here* to butcher us, they'll be caught unawares. They don't know we've escaped our chains, see. They won't know what's coming. It's our only chance at getting the hell out of here."

So that was it. Joah wobbled on his feet, dizzy from the buzzing in his ears. Aoif Deckler was still playing hero. The disappearance of half his community would have looked suspicious to the rest —had perhaps been too suspicious *last* time—so he had developed a new plan with King Isce. One that involved his own acting skills. He had been kidnapped with the rest of his people, dragged to this cellar, and locked inside. He had freed his own prisoners from their chains and helped them develop a plan of escape.

But Deckler wasn't planning on winning. *He* would survive, along with a few witnesses, who would report back to the rest of the community that their dear, valiant general had done everything he could to rescue them from the nighttime monsters.

Joah wanted to scream. To curse. To charge at his ex-boss.

He couldn't move. Misla was a statue beside him, and Damien had frozen in his mother's arms. General Deckler's voice hissed inside his head, stabbing him with needles of pain.

It's no good, Joah. Your little plan. Forget it, and you can be one of the few that live.

Joah closed his eyes, though it made no difference in the darkness. He remembered Prince Kal's words: *Don't let yourself get disoriented. Find your tongue.*

Yes, if he were to save these people from pointless butchering—if he were to convince them that Deckler was lying, that their best chance at escape was to lift the door again and stream toward the cliffs—he'd have to find his tongue.

He opened and closed his mouth, ignoring the increased muttering of the crowded bodies. Shapes emerged beneath his closed lids: he was on the High Road, surrounded by swarms of eager onlookers, but he was not leading his wife to the executioner's block. He was leading *himself*, his own handcuffs cutting into his wrists, his footsteps slow, clunky, deliberate.

"Warn you," he choked out now, opening his eyes. "Got to."

The cellar hushed. Deckler withdrew his hand from Joah's shoulder.

"What is this?" the general whispered, a cruel coldness hidden beneath his façade of shock and suspicion. "You'd like to warn us? Of what?"

"Warn you," Joah spluttered again, lurching forward.

"Scary," Damien piped up from the crook of his mother's arms.

"D-don't listen," Misla said, breathing fast. "Don't listen. Don't listen. Don't listen."

And now the muttering in the cellar rose to match the pounding buzz in Joah's ears, and somebody cried out, "They sound Infected!" and Lupita gasped and wailed.

Find your tongue, find your tongue, find your tongue, Joah begged himself, but it was too dark to find his tongue, and the prisoners were reeling, shouting insults, throwing rocks at Joah's legs. Somewhere in the back, a child wailed, and a mother said *shhh*, but the insults rose to a roar.

"Grab them," Deckler commanded. "They *are* Infected."

Damien was wrenched from his mother. Joah's wrists were pinned behind his back. He was forced to his knees between the boy and Misla, where fragments of bones stabbed his ankles, as if shattered pieces of glass coated the cellar floor. Lupita screamed.

"They'll ruin our plans," Deckler said, his voice smooth with apathy.

The prisoners responded with screeches of desperation. Joah did not blame them. They had been kidnapped by strange, scuttling creatures and forced into a cellar like pigs to a slaughterhouse. In their eyes, the Infected were threats now more than ever.

"The Nocturnals will be here any minute," Deckler said. "These three will only help them kill us. We have to get rid of them before that happens."

"*No!*" Lupita wailed, plunging forward.

Deckler ignored her, raising something into the air. As Joah's eyes finally adjusted to this new darkness, he made out the outline of a handheld saw—the same tool Deckler must have used to break the chains—bearing down upon Damien's neck.

Lupita threw herself over her son. The saw's serrated edge lodged in her neck.

"NO!" Damien roared. "MOM. NO."

Before Joah could jolt or even process what had happened, several circles of light shot into the cellar like a dozen violent stars. The outlines of a hundred Nocturnal bodies flowed into the cellar, the glowing designs on their skin glinting off the cleavers in their hands. They were cloak-less, and their figures blended together in a whirl of chaotic light.

The prisoners shrieked, bumping into each other, trying to escape like caged chickens. They had expected their kidnappers, the enslaved Leather Skins, not these new vulture-like creatures whose arms rose and fell like wings. Some tried to stab their butchers with tapered bones, but the maze of light was dizzying, and cleavers cracked into skulls with the increased rapidity of popping corn.

Joah looked up, bleary. He saw General Deckler standing in the middle of the cellar, his hacksaw dripping with Lupita's blood. He was standing shoulder-to-shoulder with a Nocturnal whose designs twisted and flared like a lair of glowing baby serpents.

King Isce grinned as he surveyed the massacre.

Find your tongue, find your tongue, find your tongue, Joah cried within himself. But it was no longer his tongue that he needed. He put his forehead to the cellar floor and let his thoughts explode, so that even some of the Nocturnals paused, their cleavers quivering in midair.

PRINCE KAL, WE NEED YOU.

His silent cry rippled through the stone of the cellar, soared against the current of the stream, weaved between foliage. It re-traveled the length of the gulley, found the starship, and embraced the cloaked figure hunkered within it.

King Isce looked up. His violet eyes narrowed when he met Joah's gaze. He had heard. He knew his long-lost heir was somewhere nearby, knew that Joah had just contacted him.

The Nocturnal king swept toward him. Joah could hear Misla gasping beside him, and Damien weeping into his mother's body, which still lay draped over the boy like a shield of flesh. He, Joah, wanted to remember his light when he finally met the dark tendrils of death.

He spread his freed hands to try to touch the woman and boy he'd come to love—

The walls shook, and *BOOM*. The world blasted apart.

A great star burst through the cellar's eastern walls, crumbling the stone and roof in a blaze of fire, exposing them to the spears of sunset's light. Prince Kal drove his ship into the ground, and it exploded on impact, sprays of sunsap flying like shards of sky.

Joah grabbed Misla and Damien, pulled them closer. Around them, King Isce's butchers clawed at blisters blossoming on their skin. King Isce himself had halted; his skin was blackening, falling to the floor in scabbed flakes as the sunset pierced him.

The king half-turned, seeming to realize, too late, what his son had done.

Kill him, he murmured.

Then his body crumbled. It collapsed into a heap of ash on the floor. And all around him, his soldiers crumbled too, until all that remained were piles of ashes, the mangled bodies of prisoners, and a handful of survivors wailing through the smoke and dust.

General Deckler himself swayed on the spot. Joah groped for his fallen rod, which lay in a heap of cinders, and aimed it at him. He was going to twist and shoot. He was going to kill the general he had obeyed and admired his whole life with a dart smothered in sunsap.

Before he could force his hands to move, Deckler's hacksaw dropped from his fingers. It landed on a pile of ashes with a soft thud. Blood spiraled around Deckler's neck. He staggered forward, then collapsed as suddenly and violently as the starship had.

Joah lowered his rod. He saw what stuck from the back of his skull, and understood.

King Isce's last command had been *kill him*. One of his butchers had stuck his cleaver into the head of the man who had failed his king. There had never been any true alliance, only a kind of hunger and greed that couldn't endure even the weakest streams of light.

"Are you okay? Are you hurt?"

Both Misla and Damien were sobbing into his chest. His own body shook as he rocked them. Deckler and Lupita were dead. King Isce had disintegrated. Prince Kal had been blasted apart. They had only managed to save a few dozen prisoners from the carnage. If they didn't get to the rest of the community soon and start sailing, that precious sun would leave them behind once again.

"It'll be okay," Joah said. "We'll find our way out of here. It'll be okay."

And he realized, despite the smoking destruction around him, that he had found his voice.

The water roared around them as the ships plunged eastward.

Joah stood beneath the foremast, watching those little white stars jump along the distant horizon. The sun had become a darkened sliver, preparing to leave them behind forever. But they hadn't let it completely shrivel into darkness. As they sailed onward, it thickened and rose until the Green Sea became a twinkling pool of orange and pink and purple.

He sensed the collective gasp of those on board, the halting of progress to watch the sun's ascent. Eventually, a woman joined him, curling her fingers around the railing beside him.

"Quite the sunset, isn't it?" Misla sighed.

Her hair hung in loose waves over her shoulders. The sunbeams made her skin appear golden, her cheeks like two glowing coins. Joah put his arm around her waist, pulled her closer, and pressed his lips against her temple. A long journey still stretched before them, but he felt peace—maybe even a little excitement—that they would cross this sea together.

"Yes, it's quite the sunset," he agreed.

"It's not a sunset anymore." Damien had appeared on Misla's other side, tiptoeing to see over the handrail. He wore a newly stitched green shirt, which had been emblazoned with the face of a reptilian cat: not just an homage to the Calic they had killed in the Eternal Night, but a reminder that darkness teemed with good *and* bad, hopeful civility *and* wild desperation. "It's technically a sun*rise*," he said. "That's what you call it when things get brighter."

"Aren't you supposed to be in school?" Joah growled.

There were a few classrooms on the lower deck for the children on board: windowless, of course, so that the students wouldn't become distracted by the sea.

"I gave Mrs. Zemukil the slip," Damien said matter-of-factly. He was barefoot, Joah noticed, his toes somehow streaked with dirt. As usual. "I wanted to see it. The dawn."

"And how'd you manage to give your teacher the slip?" Misla asked, folding her arms.

"Oh, I just passed Timby Jenkins a note. No big deal." When Misla cocked a threatening eyebrow, he added, "It was a dare, that's all. I bet him he couldn't burp a hundred times within the next arcsec. Well, Mrs. Zemukil had to stop writing on the board after his seventh burp. By his twentieth, she was yelling too hard to notice me sneak away."

Joah tried not to chuckle, but his mouth twitched.

"Watch out, Misla," he warned as the breeze picked up, smacking his face with salt. "This kid's going to be general one day. Mark my words."

They hadn't elected a new general yet. After Joah and Misla had explained to the remaining prisoners in the cellar about Deckler's arrangement with King Isce, they had agreed that escaping the fortress and boarding these ships were more pressing matters. But one of the survivors, a certain Captain Lincoln, had assumed temporary command, and *he* was the one who had convinced the rest of the Sunsetters of the truth, even with the community in disarray: between the attack on the Dirt Slums, the disappearance of their general, and a horde of Leather Skins swarming one of their three ships and taking off with it, they had been in an uproar.

But Captain Lincoln had calmed them. He had told them the truth in a giant assembly by the *shoosh* of waves, organized the remaining ships' takeoffs, and arranged for the planting of their

Nocturnal seeds onboard. There weren't any penned animals aboard—no, that would've reminded them all too much of their own recent captivity—but a garden arena on the main deck sprouted with various squashes and herbs, reminding Joah of Prince Kal and the other Nocturnals who had chased them around the aro to warn them of the darkness ahead.

"I hope Queen Usai gets our message," Misla murmured, as if she could read his thoughts. Maybe a small part of her still could, although all three of them had lost their sense of the soundless Nocturnal language, like water leaking through outspread hands.

"She will," Joah assured her.

While Captain Lincoln had been busy organizing the ships, Joah and Misla had snuck into the main, unguarded fortress, where they'd found a young cloaked Nocturnal hovering near a window. With their last remaining telepathic breath, they had told her to wait for her new Majesty, a queen by the name of Usai, who would soon come along to resume King Isce's place.

The Nocturnal had taken flight, cloak flapping behind her as she raced down the hall and disappeared around a corner. But Joah had sensed the delight squirming beneath her terror, the understanding that King Isce was gone and the aliens would be leaving soon.

"I just hate to think of Queen Usai finding the remains of that Shooting Star," Misla said.

They all fell silent, immersing themselves in the crash of water and wind. Behind them, activities were resuming: gardeners returned to the arena, Captain Lincoln continued shouting orders, and helmsmen raced to and fro. The deck creaked with movement and life.

Joah didn't wrench his eyes from the horizon, though. The three of them deserved to see it expand, he thought, to feel the sunshine warm their faces. Their tragedies had snatched away that warmth for so long, after all. They deserved to feel daylight's ripe embrace.

So with Misla and Damien beside him, with the Eternal Night behind him, he watched the distant dawn yawn itself to life until the moon rose into its new bright sky.

See Mariah Montoya's entire novella "The Nocturnals" online at Metaphorosis.
If you liked it, leave a comment. Authors love that!
Remember to subscribe to our e-mail updates so you'll know when new stories are posted.

Copyright

Title information

Metaphorosis September 2021

ISSN: 2573-136X (online)
ISBN: 978-1-64076-207-7 (e-book)
ISBN: 978-1-64076-208-4 (paperback)

Publisher

Metaphorosis
a magazine of speculative fiction

Metaphorosis Magazine is an imprint of Metaphorosis Publishing
Neskowin, OR, USA

www.metaphorosis.com

"Metaphorosis" is a registered trademark.

Discounts available

Substantial discounts are available for educational institutions, including writing workshops. Discounts are also available for quantity purchases. For details, contact Metaphorosis at metaphorosis.com/about

Metaphorosis Publishing

Metaphorosis offers beautifully written science fiction and fantasy. Our imprints include:

Metaphorosis Magazine
Plant Based Press
Verdage

You can also find us:
@MetaphorosisMag, @MetaphorosisRev, @Metaphorosis
www.facebook.com/metaphorosis

Help keep Metaphorosis running by supporting us at
Patreon.com/metaphorosis

See more about some of our books on the following pages.

Metaphorosis
a magazine of speculative fiction

Metaphorosis is an online speculative fiction magazine dedicated to quality writing. We publish an original story every week, along with author bios, interviews, and notes on story origins.

We also publish monthly print and e-book issues, as well as yearly Best of and Complete anthologies.

Come and see us online at magazine.Metaphorosis.com

Metaphorosis: Best of 2020

The best science fiction and fantasy stories from *Metaphorosis* magazine's fifth year.

Metaphorosis 2020

All the stories from *Metaphorosis* magazine's fifth year. Fifty-two great SFF stories.

Metaphorosis: Best of 2019

The best science fiction and fantasy stories from *Metaphorosis* magazine's fourth year.

Metaphorosis 2019

All the stories from *Metaphorosis* magazine's fourth year. Fifty-two great SFF stories.

Metaphorosis:
Best of 2018

The best science
fiction and fantasy
stories from
Metaphorosis
magazine's third
year.

Metaphorosis
2018

All the stories
from *Metaphorosis*
magazine's third
year. Fifty-two
great SFF stories.

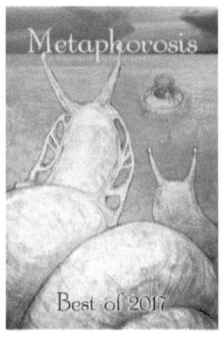 

Metaphorosis: Best of 2017

The best science fiction and fantasy stories from *Metaphorosis* magazine's *second* year.

Metaphorosis 2017

All the stories from *Metaphorosis* magazine's second year. Fifty-three great SFF stories.

Metaphorosis: Best of 2016

The best science fiction and fantasy stories from *Metaphorosis* magazine's first year.

Metaphorosis 2016

Almost all the stories from *Metaphorosis* magazine's first year.

Plant Based Press

plant
based
press

Vegan-friendly science fiction and fantasy, including an annual anthology of the year's best SFF stories.

Best Vegan SFF of 2020

The best vegan-friendly science fiction and fantasy stories of 2020!

Best Vegan SFF of 2019

The best vegan-friendly science fiction and fantasy stories of 2019!

Best Vegan SFF of 2018

The best vegan-friendly science fiction and fantasy stories of 2018!

Best Vegan SFF of 2017

The best vegan-friendly science fiction and fantasy stories of 2017!

Best Vegan SFF of 2016

The best vegan-friendly science fiction and fantasy stories of 2016!

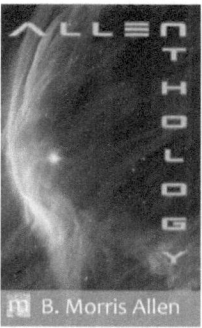

Susurrus

A darkly romantic
story of magic,
love, and
suffering.

**Allenthology:
Volume I**

A quarter century
of SFF, including
the full contents of
the collections
*Tocsin, Start with
Stones,* and
Metaphorosis.

Verdage

Science fiction and fantasy books for writers – full of great stories, often with an additional focus on the craft of speculative fiction writing.

Reading 5X5 x2

Duets

How do authors' voices change when they collaborate?

A round-robin of five talented science fiction and fantasy authors collaborating with each other and writing solo.

Including stories by Evan Marcroft, David Gallay, J. Tynan Burke, L'Erin Ogle, and Douglas Anstruther.

Score

an SFF symphony

What if stories were
written like music?
Score is an anthology
of varied stories
arranged to follow an
emotional score from
the heights of joy to
the depths of despair
– but always with a
little hope shining
through.

Reading 5X5

Five stories, five times

Twenty-five SFF authors, five base stories, five versions of each – see how different writers take on the same material.

Reading 5X5

Writers' Edition

Two extra stories, the story seed, and authors' notes on writing. Over 100 pages of additional material specifically aimed at writers.

Vestige

Novelettes, novellas, and novels by Metaphorosis authors.